Blitzkrieg Pacific

Max Lamirande

FOREWORD

The Blitzkrieg Pacific series is a work of fiction on the Second World War, where subtle differences made for a very different conflict. The book bridges the story's gap for the Pacific side and continues the Blitzkrieg Alternate storyline. It is set during the *Battle Europa timeline (book 2)* and ranges from January 1942 to June 1942.

This is the story of the Japanese offensive operations to conquer the Pacific. It also introduces new heroes to the story, as much on the American side as on the Japanese.

I have always wanted to write a book about the war in the Pacific. I've read many novels on the subject, tons of history books, and, most importantly, "wargamed" the thing countless times. This book is a direct result of that, and while I am at it, I cannot ignore the great help that Gary Grigsby's Pacific War game, a 1992 strategy wargame released by SSI, gave me in writing this book. The game spanned the war as a whole and gave me great insight into what the Japanese could have done strategically compared to their historical successes.

As my dear readers, you will enjoy the result of all those years I have mentally imagined that book.

As an introduction (this book can be read as a standalone novel), I thought that the reader might like a little of the story detailed in the book "Blitzkrieg Europa." So here it is:

World events leading up to December 1941 for the Pacific Theater. Also read: Blitzkrieg Europa book

The war that will be described in this book was a lot different than the one that unfolded historically in the Pacific. It was affected by different events in Europe, where the United Kingdom had fallen, Metropolitan France was completely occupied, and the Axis was master of the Suez Canal and the Middle East.

Because of these momentous events, America and the Soviet Union did not wait to be attacked but instead joined the war on the side of the Allies. The Americans because the fall of the UK was a wake-up call, and the Soviets because the presence of Axis troops at their all-important Caucasus oilfields was unacceptable.

The United States attention was on European events; less pressure was thus put on the Japanese government to end its war of conquest in China and along Asia. The U.S. Navy was even partially transferred to the Atlantic to react to the new threat and the fact that America was now at war with the Axis.

But with the way Japan was, and how its leader managed their war of conquest, events came to a head anyway in the Pacific. They were just delayed a little. Pearl Harbor was still targeted by Japan, but with the

American Pacific forces' reduction, the Nipponese attack was of a different scale and objectives.

This is the story of a very different Pacific War, one where Japan rides its Blitzkrieg wave for a lot longer and with a lot more aggressivity than historically.

Read on.

PROLOGUE

From its small island of Honshu, Japan desired to be the arbiter and master of Asia and the Western Pacific. The wish was born out of poverty and pride, finding company in thoughts, which made it seem just. The Japanese people even concluded that their beloved empire's expansion was natural and destined.

-General Douglas MacArthur

December 7th, 1941

President Roosevelt was sitting in the Oval Office, deep in thought. In front of him, the report on the Middle Eastern debacle was fresh on his mind. They had not been ready to fight the Axis on even terms. He knew it when he sent the troops abroad in Egypt and Iraq. But it wasn't like he'd had a choice. Not doing anything would have meant giving up on his British ally. The world was now a very uncertain place for Democracy. France and the United Kingdom were occupied, and the Fascist dictatorships were on the offensive everywhere.

The disasters had started with the surprise defeat of the French military forces in a sweeping German campaign, destroying France in mere weeks. Then came the invasion of the British Islands, again ending with a resounding German victory.

Roosevelt had then decided to intervene and attack the Axis. Even with a somewhat isolationist population, he'd had to do something to help the Free World. What followed were more defeats. First in Egypt, the Suez Canal, and then in the Middle East. It had taken a lot of political wranglings and a petition to Congress for a declaration of war, but he'd achieved it. The U.S. was now in the conflict.

The net result of the 1940-1941 campaign was that the Axis towered over all of Europe to the Soviet border and reigned supreme in the Middle East all the way to Persia. North Africa was also a Fascist realm.

Taking his cigarette from the ashtray, he took a long drag and quickly smashed it back down in a puff of swirling smoke. By god, he would beat the Nazis, he thought bitterly.

He recalled his meeting with General Marshall earlier in the day. The commander-in-chief of the armed forces had given him the figures. By the end of 1942, America would be able to field fifty divisions, ten of them armored. The madly gearing up Canadian forces would also provide twenty-five, including five armored. To his surprise, five of them would be French-Canadian, even if the civilian population used (before the fall of the United Kingdom) to be firmly against mass conscription.

The fleet would eventually be a great thing to see. Not much would come out of the shipyards early in 1942, but Roosevelt was confident that, for the moment, they could field more hulls than the Germans and Italians anyway.

He was optimistic about eventual victory, but so much work and death were still needed to make it happen, it almost made him dizzy. His only real worry was figuring out what the Japanese would do. Tokyo was part of the Axis Alliance but stayed quite preoccupied with the Chinese war.

After their occupation of French Indochina, things had been heating up between the USA and Japan lately. Tokyo had decided to move into the territory since it was a French colony. He had immediately ordered to freeze of all Japanese assets in the country, hurting them. Roosevelt knew that war with Japan was unavoidable and, in a sense, wanted it to happen.

In front of him was the executive order he was a little nervous about signing: A complete oil embargo on Japan. The disaster in the Middle East meant that the Allies would be catastrophically stupid to continue selling oil to the Axis amidst its own dwindling supplies. Because the Japanese were allied with Germany, the U.S. President would have loved to declare war on Tokyo, but things didn't work like that in a Democracy.

The country and its public opinion were now fixated on European events, and it would take a miracle to get Congress to declare war on Japan. While at war with the Third Reich, the U.S. still had isolationists within its political system. *"Hell,"* he thought sourly. Many Democrats were unhappy with the war in Europe, even if it was obvious it needed to be waged. His move against Japan could be seen as a provocation, and his political opponents would use this against him if Japan reacted aggressively.

He hesitated a little more and then decided to sign. He wrote his signature on the paper in one broad stroke. The document meant almost assured war with Tokyo since the Japanese leadership would be faced with an impossible choice. While he didn't like to think about what the Republicans would do about this, his feelings about a conflict with Japan did not overly worry him.

Intelligence assessments of the Japanese military all talked of a quick war that the Imperial forces couldn't win—a paper tiger of a sort. Roosevelt had asked more questions on the matter, particularly on the size of the Imperial Navy, which seemed more extensive than the U.S. Pacific Fleet. Admiral Kimmel, the commander-in-chief of the Navy in the Pacific, had told him not to worry and that the boys would make short work of the tiny Asian men. Like most Western countries, the Americans didn't take the Japanese fighting men (or its government's will) seriously.

He figured that the Philippines and Guam would be in grave danger, but those were outlying territories, and besides, the U.S. had forces there with General Douglas MacArthur in command. No one in the intelligence or military circles believed the Japanese could hit America or even beat their troops in Asia. After all, the British also had substantial troops there; the Allies had Australian forces, the Dutch, and the New Zealanders. Finally, Japan was stuck in a continental war with China. Thus, no one in Washington believed they could successfully wage war in the Pacific against the world's most prominent industrial power.

He looked at the signed paper one last time, hesitating slightly. He believed in doing something against the Japanese but wasn't certain things would go as well as the military had told him. He called an aide to come pick up the executive document. Turning his wheelchair around to look at the beautiful garden, he lit another cigarette, taking a satisfying breath.

All would be well, he finally convinced himself.

National Diet Building, December 8th, 1941

If only Roosevelt had known.

No one in America understood what the Japanese were capable of. None thought their government was crazy enough to believe they could conquer the World with their Axis allies.

None believed that they could put the whole Pacific Ocean afire and conquer, in what seemed the blink of an eye, most of it to threaten the very core of the United States and Australia. But in a sense, the Western World should have been paying attention to the pace of Japanese expansion and the sheer will it showed while doing it.

As newly minted Prime Minister Hideki Tojo dropped the piece of paper in front of him, he re-adjusted his small round glasses. It was the report from Imperial HQ on the new presidential order forbidding oil deliveries to the Empire. He sat up and moved away from his desk, crossing his arms between his back, lost in thought.

The man was dressed in his Imperial Army general's uniform (as always). He had close-cropped hair, a black mustache, and round spectacles. He was in a small, austere office (as he liked it) in the National Diet Building, where the politicians met in Japan, and the Office of the Prime Minister was located. There was an official residence in Tokyo, but Tojo had not used it yet.

The man had been, before his ascension to Prime Minister, a prominent figure in the Kwantung Army and was crucial in opening hostilities against China in 1937. And he was now the man who would lead Japan into the war against the biggest and most powerful country on earth.

Because from the moment he dropped the paper on the table in front of him, he'd decided he would do what was needed for the Empire's destiny to continue forward. He also knew that all of the men and leaders around him would follow his lead.

He looked absently at nothing in particular for a few moments. The Americans had dared defy Japan. They'd dared cut the flow of oil, steel, and their assets. They were giving Japan only two options. Witter on the vine or war with America.

He picked up the phone right with his left hand. *"Yes, Prime Minister,"* said one of his aides on the other side of the line. *"Call an Imperial Council,"* was all he said before adding, *"for tonight." "Yes, Prime Minister."*

Extract from General Macarthur's book, Reminiscences, 1964

The gathering storm

I have been involved in man's greatest conflict to date and, as such, have been privileged to play a significant role in its conclusion. With this book, I hope to be able to explain my perspective as an American leader and general.

In 1937 (in my capacity as the commander-in-chief of all armed forces in the Philippines), I accompanied Quezon, the Filipino leader, when he visited Japan, the United States, and Mexico. The visit to the land of the rising sun was particularly instructive for the conflagration that was to follow. It wasn't really hard to see that the chicken would come to roost at one point.

Confined on its four main islands with a large population and not enough resources, Japan could barely feed its demographically expanding population. The Japanese lacked sugar, and thus, the imperial military went for Formosa and conquered it. Then, they needed iron for their increasing military and burgeoning industry, and thus, they went for Manchuria. They needed more security, so they took Korea.

And yet, after all these conquests, they still lacked the hard coal, and the timber, and so they went for China. Once that was achieved, they needed strategic metals like nickel and oil from Southeast Asia, and the Dutch East Indies. Since those territories were controlled by Western Powers (England,

France. USA, and the Netherlands), one didn't need to be a prophet to see the writing on the wall.

By 1941 and in early 1942, not utterly blind to Japanese military ambitions, the U.S. Government finally acted. European events took an ominous turn, and Roosevelt got Congress to declare war on the Germans. By the time Guderian pushed back our last forces from the Middle East and defeated General Clark, events were also coming to a boil in Asia. The Sino-Japanese war was in full swing, and there seemed to be no end in sight. The Japs also had just occupied French Indochina, which had been the last warning for us. Tokyo was not going to stop on its war logic.

With this state of affairs, the U.S. Government finally decided to re-instate me as a full general in the United States military. On July 27th, I received a second cable from General George Marshall (the Army chief-of-staff, or commander in chief of all U.S. armed forces):

"Effective this date, a command designated as the United States Army Forces in the Far East is hereby constituted. This command will include the Philippine Department, forces of the Commonwealth of the Philippines called into the service of the armed forces of the United States for the period of the existing emergency, and such other forces as may be designated to it. The Headquarters of the United States Army Forces in the Far East will be established in Manila, Philippine Islands. You are hereby designated as Commanding General United States Army Forces in the Far East."

Little did I know that this command would define my life and bring me to manage the biggest conflict the Pacific will ever see.

Meeting, December 14th, 1941

A few days after receiving the American oil embargo and upon Tojo's summon, the Japanese Imperial Navy and Army leaders were busy surveying a map of a small chain of islands in the middle of the Pacific. Admiral Yamamoto and General Tojo were overlooking the Island of Oahu. They just finished absorbing most of the military intelligence reports. They also had all the information they needed on American ships' whereabouts in the headlines. The Americans pushed them all the way to the abyss with their oil embargo. For all instances and purposes, this meant that Japan had only six months left of oil for its military. The Japanese leadership was thus faced with two choices. Evacuate China and Indochina or continue on its war logic.

The choice was not really difficult for these proud men. While they were wary of a conflict with the American giant, they were also supremely confident in the superiority of the Japanese fighting man and the spirit of Bushido. Conveniently for them, the USA had transferred its three operational carriers, two of the four battleship divisions, and several cruiser squadrons to the Atlantic in their war against the European Axis. Oahu was almost defenseless.

This represented a golden opportunity for Japan. The major harbor of Pearl Harbor, the central naval base for the Americans in the Pacific, was laid open for an attack. Moreover, the Americans had also removed two brigades from the Island Chain for their campaign in the Middle East against Germany. This convinced Admiral Yamamoto that Oahu and the other islands could be invaded and occupied, thus inflicting a severe blow to the USA in the Pacific and on its ability to wage war against Japan. It took him a little time to convince the Army (ever focused on the Chinese war) to supply the landing troops and the supplies.

But in the end, he wanted the Prime Minister's (General Tojo) support, and here they were, looking at the timetable for their operation. America was in for a surprise.

The Pearl Harbor attack was only the opening salvo and a tiny part of a large-scale offensive across the Pacific. Over the next few weeks, the Imperial Army and Navy would plan for attacks against the Philippines, British Malaya (Singapore), the Dutch East Indies, and several islands in the Pacific.

"Grand Admiral Yamamoto," said Field Marshal Hajime Sugiyama, the commander of the Imperial Army. *"Are you certain that the attack on Pearl Harbor can succeed and that the troops the Army supplies you with will be sufficient?"* "Field Marshal," answered the Grand Admiral. *"It is not a matter of if it can succeed. It must succeed, and for that matter, this is why I have asked the Army for three of its elite divisions in order to land in force and overwhelm the ten thousand or so American soldiers on the island chain."*

The Army commander wasn't satisfied with the Navy man's answer. He was still unhappy about the idea of landing troops so far from Japan. *"Wouldn't these forces be better used in our coming operations in the Pacific and Southeast Asia?"* It was a fact that the operation was risky and that holding the Hawaiian Islands would prove a major undertaking for the Empire. At the same time, Japan would have its hands full with conquering the territories and resources it needed. After all, it had already been fighting to the death with China since 1937 and had millions of soldiers in continental Asia. *"I fear we will be over-extending ourselves,"* added the Army field marshal again.

"Marshal Hajime," answered Yamamoto, using an exasperated tone. *"Conquering the Pacific is one thing; keeping the Americans and Allies from retaking it will be another. Do you know who we will fight against once we destroy its fleet in Hawaii?"* The Army commander-in-chief didn't answer because he knew the answer. *"The United States is the biggest industrial power on earth. I have lived in the USA. Believe me, once we smash their fleet in Pearl, we better be in the fight for the duration."* The Grand Admiral paused again, putting his finger on the map exactly where Oahu was located. *"The Hawaiian Islands are the most powerful and only naval base from which the Americans can attack us. As long as we hold it, they will not be able to project their power in the rest of the Pacific, thus safeguarding Japan's conquest and giving us the time to prepare for the unavoidable U.S. reconquest campaign."*

Tojo didn't like what Yamamoto had just predicted. The politician decided to intervene in the discussion. *"Admiral, your lack of confidence in Japanese might be disconcerting."* Sugiyama was of the same mind. *"I agree, Mr. Prime Minister. Why should the Army give the Navy three good divisions for such an operation with a leader so bent on thinking or imagining the Empire's defeat or our enemy's might?"*

The Japanese strategic mind took a deep breath. These men didn't understand what they were faced with. They were locked in their conception of the world based on what they knew and their beliefs. Japan was, after all, a very small island; thus, it was hard for men like Tojo and the Marshal to imagine something as powerful as the United States of America.

Yamamoto had studied in the United States. He'd seen the large industrial cities, the vastness of the country's resources—and the innumerable numbers of its population.

But most importantly, its national character. By storming the Hawaiian Islands and launching a war of conquest across the Pacific Sea, he knew full well that he would wake up a sleeping giant. But alas, his countrymen were bent on continuing their war logic, and he was only a faithful servant of the Empire. He'd tried to convince them to try and deal with the Yankees but had failed.

"Gentlemen, we need to invade Hawaii and thus protect our flank from the vengeful Americans. By sinking the fleet anchored in Pearl Harbor and taking over the Islands, we could fortify it and block the U.S. Navy from attacking our other possessions in the Pacific theater. We will also be free to act as we please for as long as we hold Oahu and its harbor." Looking at the two men facing him, he paused and finished with all the seriousness he could muster: *"I shall run wild considerably for the first six months or a year, but I have utterly no confidence for the second and third year. I fear all we will do by starting this war will be to awaken a colossus and, unfortunately, fill him with a terrible resolve."*

Tojo and Sugiyama, impervious to anything running contrary to their dreams of conquest and wishful thinking, did not appreciate the seriousness of Yamamoto's bold statement. The Empire's manifest destiny was at hand, and it was time to attack.

Thus, they ignored the Grand Admiral's prophecy.

Extract of Tameichi Hara's book Teikoku Kaigun no Saigo 1967

Combined fleet gathering in Hiroshima Bay, January 11th, 1942

January 11th, 1942, is an unforgettable day for me. The entire Imperial Combined Fleet was assembled in Kure Harbor and the adjoining bay that day. For such a gathering to happen meant that truly momentous events were upon us. I was captain of the destroyer Amatsukaze, recently included in the Second Fleet's destroyer squadron.

It was a beautiful winter day, cold and crisp but sunny. All the Imperial Navy vessels lay unmoving on the mirror-like surface of the sea. The water was so still it reflected the mountains on the faraway skyline. Seagulls flew over us in their usual banter. Looking at the scene, I was peaceful but wary of what would happen.

Orders soon came down by flag signals to gather on the Yamato, the Combined Fleet's flagship. *"All commanding officers will report to the flagship."* My motor launch carried me toward the super battleship a few minutes later. Its incredibly large stern accommodated all the few hundred officers that gathered for the occasion.

When everyone was seemingly on the battlewagon, three bells sounded across Yamato, signaling all crew members to leave the decks only to ship captains or lieutenant commanders rank and above. The unusual precaution only served to increase the tension we all felt.

And then Admiral Yamaguchi, one of the combined fleet HQ commanders, shouted from the podium above all of us, installed near one of the anti-aircraft turret platforms that the super dreadnought sported. *"Gentlemen, attention, please! The Commander-in-Chief will be here in a moment."*

We all stood at attention as Grand Admiral Isoroku Yamamoto appeared on deck. He strode to the podium and started speaking. *"Thank you all for coming to Yamato for this briefing. Our combined fleet has completed preparations for war. We will continue training on that basis."* The Grand Admiral paused for effect and gave us all a comprehensive look. *"It appears that the Western Powers are not giving us a lot of choice. Japan may be forced to take up arms against America, Britain, Australia, and the Netherlands rather than succumb to strangulation through their economic blockade."* He readjusted his cap for good measure. *"If war is declared, the Combined Fleet will have to face its most serious conflict to date. Once our leader decides on war, our brave ships and sailors must fight and vanquish our enemies. We have trained for this for years. We have built the ships; thus, this task is doable, but only if we work hard and proficiently toward that goal. The Empire expects each of you to do your duty with me so we can fulfill our destiny."*

The Grand Admiral's words echoed in the still silence of the bay around us and blazed through our conscious minds. We were to fight not only the Americans, but the British, and the Dutch and who else? He then stopped his speech, looking at each of his frozen and stunned officers. Then, he gave us a formal military salute and left the podium for Admiral Yamaguchi again.

Then, the gravity of the situation dawned on us as Yamaguchi explained the details. The Allied embargo was choking Japan on critical resources such as oil, iron, rubber, zinc, tin, nickel, and bauxite. This put our continued offensive into China in jeopardy, as well as the Navy's continued operational capabilities. Thus, the Emperor had taken the decision to strike back at the Allied stranglehold strategy. Yamaguchi's last words to us, which were heavy in meaning, left me somewhat apprehensive about the future: *"This grand gathering is the first and might be the last, gentlemen. We may not be able to see each other in this fashion ever again..."*

I remained stunned for the whole day after the meeting as Yamamoto and Yamaguchi's words rang in my ears for a long time.

Sailing toward destiny, February 27th, 1942

The sizeable Japanese carrier was rolling over the giant waves, splashing sea water around. Minoru Genda, Akagi's squadron leader, looked at the setting sun over the horizon. It had been another dull day on the great ship. There was not even one patrol in the skies as the Combined Fleet sailed toward Pearl Harbor and its destiny.

The fleet followed a complicated sailing pattern, avoiding known atolls and islands in the Central Pacific (by a considerable margin) to advance toward Hawaii in total secrecy. Strict radio silence was thus observed by the ships of the Imperial Navy, and they sailed all bunched up close to each other in order to be able to communicate via flag and light signals.

As he looked at the mighty ships surrounding the superb Akagi, he pondered for a moment about what Japan was about to do. In the summer of 1940, he went to Europe as a military observer and saw the capabilities of the German and British fighters in action during the Battle of England.

His conclusion was that the Japanese Mitsubishi A6M Zero could easily outperform anything both of them fielded at the time (Spitfire, Hurricanes, and Bf-109s. He'd seen the inferiority of their future enemy's machines but, at the same time, the resilience of their fighting men. He wasn't too confident it was the best of ideas to go and surprise them with that big of an attack in Pearl Harbor. It was sure to make them as mad as hell, and he suspected it would not play well for Japan in the long run.

As part of his travels, he'd seen the size of the United States and discussed it with Admiral Yamamoto. They both weren't certain tackling the industrial giant was a good idea.

Genda's Western European trip provided added stimulus (and again, he wasn't sure it was a good thing) for Japanese strategic naval studies and exercises to discover weaknesses and formulate tactics to use against the Western Allies. In short, the Japanese leaders were going into this fight confident of victory, and they might have been wise to ponder a little before getting into this vast and daunting fight.

On his return to Japan, he was named to the First Carrier Division (Akagi, Kaga, Soryu, and Hiryu) and met with Yamamoto in early August 1941. As relations between Japan and the United States were worsening by the day at that time, the Grand Admiral presented him with some ideas for attacking the U.S. Pacific Fleet. He confirmed to Yamamoto that an air raid with carriers on Oahu was doable. The next day, he had been named officially in charge of the pilot training for an attack on Pearl Harbor. The training included the difficult maneuver of torpedo attacks in shallow waters like the ones at the Hawaiian harbor.

And here he was, months later, with a superbly trained force of highly skilled pilots. He was confident they would make a killing in Hawaii. The men he commanded were good, tough, and, most importantly, hardened by years of war in China. All his ace pilots had several victories under their belts or some battles that had hardened their senses. The relentless training they'd been subjected to in the last year and a half had finished the polishing job.

And Minoru was right to feel this way. Imperial Japan was going to war with the finest carrier-capable air force in the world. Before attrition made its mark on it, it would dominate the skies in the Pacific and score countless victories. The U.S. airmen would have a very tall order to fulfill if they wanted to beat their Japanese opponents.

CHAPTER 1

Battleship Yamato, February 1st, 1942

Grand Admiral Isoroku Yamamoto was in his "Admiral of the Fleet" cabin aboard the largest dreadnought ever built. Yamato was a new type of dreadnought called super battleship because of its incredible displacement (72,000 tons), its thick armor, and its truly massive guns (18.1 inches).

Named after the ancient Japanese Yamato Province, the giant battlewagon and its sistership (Musashi, the second in the class, was still under construction) was formally commissioned on the first week of January 1942. The Grand Admiral could still feel the ship's pristine air about it. In fact, the battleship was sailing on its first official cruise. The Imperial Navy was conducting exercises in the vicinity of Iwo Jima Island in order to practice the coming operation on Pearl Harbor.

The last month had been some of the most work-intensive weeks in Yamamoto's life. And rightly so, as the Empire was about to embark on the greatest endeavor it ever had in attempting to conquer all of the Pacific and Southeast Asia. The country needed the resources, manpower, and living space to expand its military, feed its population, and develop its industrial infrastructure.

The plan called for several main trusts to attack almost simultaneously and had taken a lot of time to coordinate. At that moment, troops, ships, and planes still moved about to prepare for the incredible campaign.

First and foremost, the main attack would involve a full invasion of the Hawaiian Islands, with the twin objectives of sinking the U.S. Pacific fleet's leftovers and occupying the Island chain to shield Japan's position against the Americans.

Yamamoto didn't know how long he would hold out against America. Still, he was confident that by taking control of the only harbor within a 3000-miles radius, he ensured that he would know where the enemy would come from. The U.S. Navy could not contemplate any Pacific reconquest without Hawaii, especially since Yamamoto had also planned to launch operations at American Samoa and French New Caledonia, the only two passably suitable deep-water harbors before Australia.

Once he took control of Oahu and the other islands, he would build numerous new airfields and fortifications and cram them with troops and planes. His plan also involved the stationing of the Combined Fleet directly in Oahu. As long as the large Imperial Navy defended the Islands, Yamamoto was certain he could keep the Americans at bay for a long while. He even envisioned naval raids on the American mainland, which would contribute to keeping the enemy off-balance even more.

The attack was to have several major Army / Navy groups, each with a different set of objectives. Japan certainly needed the Dutch East Indies for its oil, rubber, and other resources, so he'd slated a lot of troops and ships toward that part of the campaign. Then, the Philippines could not be ignored because of their strategic position in the center of the future Japanese Empire. There was also the fact that the Americans were based there and entertained troops and planes on Luzon (the main island).

The British possessions in Southeast Asia could not be ignored either, so more troops had been planned for that. First and foremost, the Japanese Army needed to take Singapore, the famed British fortress in Malaya. The city was strategically located at the tip of Asia proper and could not be ignored. Another large army was being moved toward French Indochina and from southern China in preparation for an offensive toward Burma, another country with oil and other essential resources.

Finally, the Grand Admiral had organized a series of intricate and smaller-scale invasions of dozens upon dozens of tiny Pacific Islands, ranging from American Samoa to the most miniature atolls in the Gilbert Islands or even the Island of Wake, halfway between Japan and Pearl Harbor. With these, he hoped he would control all of the sea lanes in the Pacific and be able to sever communication between the USA and Australia to prevent the US Navy from interfering with Japan.

The four primary attacks were organized as such:

Dutch Invasion Group (based out of Cam Rahn Bay, Indochina)

Objectives: Java and Sumatra, Celebes, Borneo and Timor

Japan needed oil, so it had been decided to put the greatest effort and speed toward the Dutch East Indies, which had plenty of the precious liquid so crucial to modern armies. The IJA (Imperial Japanese Army) 16th and the Imperial Guard Divisions, assembled in Taiwan and Japan, were ordered on January 2nd to move to Cam Ranh Bay. They became the main force of the Dutch invasion group and the Malaya invasion group. A few divisions were removed from the Kwantung Army in Manchuria (on the Sino-Soviet Border) to reinforce the attacks. Cam Rahn was located in the southern part of the newly conquered French Indo-China territory. It was a large bay with critical military installations built by the French during their colonial rule. Japan decided to take the base and use it to prepare its Southeast Invasion Group. The Dutch Invasion Group was also supplied with over 600 aircraft of all types in terms of air power.

A powerful fleet centered on the small aircraft carrier Hosho would make things happen for the Nipponese. It was also supplied with several mighty surface ships, like the trio of Yamashiro, Hyuga, and Ise battleships and five Takao/Aoba Class heavy cruisers. Twelve light cruisers and over fifty destroyers completed the screening forces for 250 transport ships.

The Dutch Invasion Group had the most intricate and complicated task of all. It involved the execution of several landings in difficult places and potential naval battles since the Allies were sure to oppose the Japanese fleet trying to land its troops).

Philippines Invasion Group (based in Taiwan and Palau Island)
Objectives: Philippines

Being much closer to the Nipponese base in Formosa and Palau Island, the Japanese invasion of the Philippines was a more straightforward campaign than the Dutch one. It involved only two major landings, one on the largest southern Island, Mindanao, and one where the main American forces resided, on Luzon Island.

None other than General Macarthur was in Manilla. He had just been named overall commander of all American Forces in Asia. So there were several U.S. divisions in the area near Luzon and also the Clark Airfield Complex. The USA entertained several squadrons of planes that could strike Formosa and attack Japanese shipping.

Yamamoto's plan, which had been organized in collaboration with the Imperial Army, called for a landing of an entire army in the north in order to confront the Americans, and two more divisions would sail from Palau, where they would quickly occupy Mindanao (and the important Davao harbor) and then move to the other smaller islands. It wasn't heavily garrisoned like Luzon.

Two strong fleets would escort the landings, with a battleship each (Haruna and Kongo) and also the Ryujo and Zhuiho aircraft carriers. Over 500 aircraft were gathered (in Formosa mostly) for the operation to smash American airpower in the theater.

Yamamoto hoped to be able to reduce American presence in the Philippines to nothing by the end of the 1942 summer. By then, the first convoys of the precious Dutch resources were planned to be conquered and re-gathered for Japanese purposes and its factories in the Home Islands.

Malaya Invasion Group

Objectives: Malaya / Singapore

The Japanese attack on British Malaya, and ultimately Singapore, was a more recognizable form of warfare in the traditional sense of the word: armies marching on land to get to an objective and taking it, except that the British didn't think that an attack would come from land.

Singapore was the strongest fortress in Asia and was deemed impregnable by most military experts. It was supplied with impressive fortifications, cannons (only facing the sea, unfortunately for the Allies), and several good units defending it.

The Japanese plan was straightforward in its simplicity. Advance an army through Thailand and down the Malay Peninsula. It was simple, and it was also something the British high command didn't think possible. The area was filled with a thick jungle infested with vermin and hostile populations. No army had gone through the area in recent history, and thus, the English felt safe in their fortress, for it was said that Singapore could withstand a duel with dozens of battleships and win.

The Japanese forces for the invasion were assembled in 1941 on Hainan Island and in French Indochina. From the island came the famed 18th Division, one of the best veteran units of the Chinese war, which had already been raging for four years. From the mainland also came several hardened units from the Chinese theater.

As Yamamoto and Hajime's staff officers planned, the key to the operation was the landing on Malaya's northern coast at Kota Bharu. The move would considerably shorten the trek through the jungle and was designed to seize as much territory as possible and impede the Allies from organizing any type of defense north of Singapore. This is where the 18th would land, along with several of the elite Japanese Marine battalions. The rest of the army would join them after they walked from Indochina to Singapore overland.

The forces would be under the stern and successful command of the soon-to-be-famous General Yamashita, who would take Singapore and sweep through Asia and Australia.

Pacific invasion group (based in Kwajalein and Truk)

Objectives: Noumea, American Samoa, Gilbert Islands Wake, Johnson Atoll New Hebrides, Solomons, New Britain.

From Yamamoto's point of view, the Pacific campaign to capture the various strategic islands was the most important. It was directed at the country he considered the main (and only) deathly threat to Imperial Japan: The United States of America. Unfortunately for the Empire, the Army and several of his fellow colleagues in the Navy disagreed with him. This meant he would not necessarily have everything he needed to prevent the U.S. Navy from returning and liberating the Pacific. But he would try to make do with what he had.

The Grand Admiral knew full well that the Empire needed Dutch oil, Borneo rubber, Chinese iron, and all the other resources. He also knew that most islands he ordered, occupied, and conquered didn't harbor any essential prizes like oil in the East Indies. Yet, those same little bits of Pacific paradises held the most important assets in his eyes: strategic positioning against whom he viewed as the main enemy.

First and foremost, he launched an operation to take Hawaii and its main harbor. Then, he planned other operations across the Pacific to prevent the Americans from building or having any deep-water ports and to block any chance of Australia being supplied easily through the shipping lanes.

The first territories in the Grand Admiral's sight were New Britain, the Gilbert Islands, Wake Island, and Johnston Atoll. Objectives further away were also targeted in the campaign—Noumea (New Caledonia), American Samoa. Even further away, the Fijis and Tahiti. If Japan could reach all those goals, it would mean more time for the country to prepare. Yamamoto hoped to stall the unavoidable American comeback and for Japan to somehow bring them to the negotiating table.

Hickam Field, Hawaii

February 28th, 1942

Lieutenant Harry Bergman finished his landing phase at Hickam Field in Oahu, Hawaii. It had been another excellent day under the Pacific sun; A friendly little patrol around Kahuku and a rendezvous over Diamond Head in a couple of exercises.

He was flying a lot more lately since the brass expected the United States to be soon at war with the Japs. In any case, he wasn't overly worried about the potential enemy. He felt safe in the faraway tropical paradise of the Hawaiian Islands.

He opened the plane's flap and received the go-ahead over the radio that it was his time to land. He eased the throttle, seemingly hovering about the airfield's tarmac for a moment, and then dropped it, touching the ground in a tire-screeching noise. He rolled all the way to the last third of the runway, where the aircraft finally stopped.

He opened the canopy and lifted himself out of the fighter. Walking on the wing momentarily, he dropped on the asphalt, gently tapping his plane. The Curtiss P-40 Warhawk was the main American fighter at the beginning of 1942. How it would fare against the Japanese models remained to be seen in the Pacific Theater. Harry wasn't overly worried about it since all Americans believed the Japs had inferior technology and fighting capabilities.

The American pilot didn't know it yet, but his beloved plane wouldn't do so well against the all-new A6M Zero fighters that the Japanese were about to unleash in the Pacific theater and (unfortunately for Bergman) in Pearl Harbor.

Politely saluting the mechanic walking toward his P-40, he continued on toward a jeep awaiting him. An orderly was at the wheel to bring him to the main barrack. A party was planned tonight at Bellows Beach, and he didn't want to miss it. He needed to make good time to get there as it was on the other side of the Island (near the Kaneohe Army base), and traffic was terrible during the day.

Oblivious to the rest, little did he know that his life was about to change.

March 1st, 1942

Admiral Isoroku Yamamoto, standing in the control tower of the mighty battleship Yamato, was pondering the last details of the "Shoho" operation. It had been a complex one to prepare, as the attack would be simultaneous across many fronts and areas across the Pacific. The Imperial Army, with the help of the Imperial Navy, would launch a general offensive against the Philippines, Malaysia, Singapore, and the Dutch East Indies, where the oil they needed was waiting to be taken.

The Dutch were weak, their homeland being occupied by the Germans. Although Churchill had sent some troops to Singapore to stiffen the defenses, the British also had the same predicament. The French were already gone from the chessboard (except for New Caledonia and Tahiti) with Japan's occupation of French Indochina several months earlier.

That left the American powerhouse needing to be neutralized. The Admiral had serious doubts about a long-term campaign against them. He studied in the USA and saw its industrial power. The United States had enormous military potential. A potential that Japan could not hope to match. In a private meeting with Tojo and the Emperor, he'd promised them six months to a year of pure Japanese domination in the Pacific, after which he did not guarantee anything. His prediction at the talks was that Japan would be on the defensive within twelve months. And that was the best-case scenario. While he had some misgivings about the coming fight, he would still prosecute it to the best of his ability. He wasn't a politician but a warrior.

The removal of two battleship divisions and all three carriers from the Pacific theater by the Americans created an opportunity for Yamamoto. One that changed his initial idea of simply launching a powerful air raid at Pearl Harbor, the main naval base in the Pacific for the US Navy. The U.S. Navy was weak in the Pacific after several of its main units had been sent to the other ocean. He did not understand why the American President had transferred so many ships in the Atlantic since the Germans had few themselves. Maybe he was afraid of the prominent and modern Italian Navy. Or else it was the typical and arrogant American behavior about their supposed superiority over Japan and Asian nations.

While he didn't harbor a lot of confidence in a global war against the USA, he was certain of one thing; His forces would show the Westerners that they could be their equals and even their betters. They would be mad as hell against Japan for the surprise attack the Grand Admiral was about to unleash, but at least they would not be arrogant anymore.

A Zero fighter thundering above him brought him back to reality. For a moment, he was back on the Yamato's bridge, looking out at the dark night with its aircraft lifting off the six great carriers that accompanied the Combined Fleet for the operation. And then he plunged back into his mind, thinking.

He had started to think about being able to land and take over the Islands because the U.S. had so weakened its position in Hawaii that they'd almost invited him to do it. If this could be achieved, he hoped -and had somewhat promised General Tojo- that he could guarantee more than a year of domination in the struggle for the Pacific. Inwardly, he dearly hoped that holding to the Hawaiian Islands would lock the Pacific in the Americans for an undetermined period of time.

Pearl Harbor, located halfway between Japan, Australia, and the many island chains in the Pacific, was the only base from which the Yankees could launch operations in the theater. Without Oahu and its major harbor, the USA would be left with only one option: Retake the Islands chain before doing anything else. Yamamoto had high hopes for defending them, as well-prepared Hawaiian Islands could be a true fortress if bolstered by the main elements of the Imperial Navy. If they could hold on, then maybe Japan would have a chance of winning the war.

Deep in his thoughts, he was pulled back into reality again by the gentle bow of a deck officer who slowly gestured toward the fleet carriers, where the faint lights of the many planes were taking off to the skies. It was one hour before dawn on the 1st of March 1942. The lights seemed to stretch in a long line toward the horizon. There were six long columns of planes going toward Hawaii. Their plane lights on a dying night created a nice view. The aircraft were taking off from the decks of the six main fleet carriers: Akagi, Shokaku, Zuikaku, Hyriu, Soryu, and Kaga.

Over 400 planes would hit Pearl Harbor and the military airports on Oahu. From a bird's eye view, the assembled Japanese fleet was enormous. In the center were the six crucial carriers. On every side, six of the Navy's battleships were flanking them, as well as eight heavy cruisers, fifteen light cruisers, and plenty of destroyers. The whole naval formation was stretching for miles on end. Further out in front was a screen of submarines to warn the fleet of any impending American fleet. Five hundred miles further back sailed the troop transports that would come in once the Imperial Navy had pounded most of the American defenses to scraps.

Yamamoto was not overly worried about an enemy reaction since the Americans had no known aircraft carriers or any substantial naval force in the area. If the three battleships reported to be in Pearl Harbor decided to make a sortie (he didn't believe they would have time before the planes arrived), they would be met by the big guns of the Imperial Navy, with his own ship in front.

Yamato was the biggest battleship in the world, with 457mm (18.1 in.) guns and 72 800 tons of displacement at full load. It was the first of a series of four super-battleships (the second, Musashi, was scheduled to be launched in the middle of 1942), designed to slug it out with the American fleet. It was so large that it was wider than some of the docks in the Panama Canal. So if the U.S. Navy wanted to build ships as big as the Japanese, they would not be able to cross the Panama Canal but need to go around the Cape Horn in Chile, adding several weeks to any wanted ships transfer in the Pacific.

It took several minutes for all the planes to take off, assemble, and then head toward Pearl Harbor. The admiral hoped for a devastating first strike.

All across the Pacific, roughly at the same time, given the time difference, Japanese forces sprung out from their starting positions and pounced on Allied airfields, ships, and other facilities.

The war in the Pacific had started, and it wasn't about to end anytime soon.

The Pearl Harbor attack
Minoru Genda, March 1st, 1942

As the big ship sailed up desperately to exit the harbor, Genda lined up facing it. The battleship Nevada was harassed on all sides, firing its flak left to right, high and low, against the Japanese planes buzzing about it. The anti-aircraft ordinance's red tracers filled the skies around in some macabre firecracker show. Several fires raged on its deck, as it had been gutted by several bombs already. Water gushed inside from a deep gouge from one of the Val planes (the Aichi D3A Type 99 Carrier Bomber) bombs that had been able to hit it earlier.

The scene was a catastrophic maelstrom of fire and explosion, flak ordinance climbing in the air, and Japanese planes flying around, firing their cannon shells, dropping their torpedoes at ships in the harbor, or else unleashing their bombs either on the airfields or even the other US vessels at anchorage.

Earlier in the day, the Japanese airstrike was a complete surprise to the still-sleeping Americans. The 400 aircraft had flown low over the sea to avoid detection, and at first, most of the U.S. lookouts in the harbor and on the ships didn't recognize them for what they were. Not many in the USA had thought it possible that the enemy could attack them in their safe Pearl Harbor base; it was so far away from everything and so much of a paradise that it just didn't register to most as a dangerous place.

But as America stood against Japanese ambition in Asia and the Pacific, all logic had pointed to it being at the forefront of a war between the two nations. On March 1st, 1942, it witnessed the birth of the most significant conflict that the Pacific would ever see in its history.

The Nipponese air swarm plunged on the US Navy, the harbor, and the airfields around Oahu. The first attack was devastating. The battleship Arizona was one of the first to go up in a catastrophic explosion, with several bombs from Val planes straddling its deck in the first half-minute of the attack. In what would be explained later as a "shell magazine containment failure," the ship was rocked by a gigantic explosion, almost splitting it in two, lifting the great ship in the air, for it to settle back down cracked like an egg, spilling fire and smoke, spurting metal debris in every direction. The dreadnought was a total loss from that very moment, and most of its sailors were dead. The great plume of smoke it created as it continued to burn as a vortex of fire rose high in the sky, even obscuring the Japanese pilots' views to target other ships.

Genda expertly moved his plane's stick to stabilize his Nakajima BN5 torpedo bomber to drop its weapon into the water and finish the American battleship trying to sail out of Pearl. Below the plane was its Type 91 torpedo, designed to be used specifically in harbors with shallow water depth. Some anti-aircraft fire was coming his way, as the gun servant in Nevada had seen him and tried to explode him out of the sky. He finally loosed his weapon into the water, his plane climbing a few meters instantly in altitude because of the weight it was released from.

Genda then banked his BN5 hard left while pulling back on his plane stick, so his bomber climbed rapidly in the sky. The flak tried to follow him, and red tracers with dark explosions filled his wake in sequence, but Nevada's gunners never adjusted in time to catch Minoru's aircraft climbing in the sky.

And then, seconds later, the torpedo hit directly in the front of the ship, igniting a catastrophic explosion that rocked the battleship to its core and stopped it dead in its tracks. Its bow lifted up in the air for a moment and then plunged back into the sea, taking a significant amount of water from the new, large gap the Japanese weapon had created. More explosions happened in a chain of events, putting most of the ship's frontal part on fire. As Genda circled over the boat half a minute after his climb, he could see that the Nevada was done for and decided to go back to base to rearm; he'd expanded most of the B5M's ammo anyway and needed a new torpedo.

Approaching Windward side, Oahu, March 1st, 1942

The Japanese 46 cm/45 (18.1 in) Type 94 naval gun was the largest ever mounted on a warship. And during the developing conflict that was just opening up with the Pearl Harbor attack, it would prove its power on many occasions. In 1942, only Yamato carried them, but two more ships were planned to have them, the Musashi (nearing completion in Japan) and the Shinano, in the early stages of construction. But in the end, only the Imperial Japanese Navy's World War II super-battleships Yamato and Musashi fired these guns in anger, for the Shinano would eventually be modified as an aircraft carrier later in the war to compensate for Japanese losses at sea.

The gun was designed following the prevailing Japanese naval strategy of Kantai Kessen, or the "Decisive Battle Doctrine." The idea was to bring the enemy fleet to battle, destroy it, and win the war in one fight, like at Tsushima, when the Japanese Empire had defeated the larger Russian Baltic Fleet and ended the war in one fell swoop. No other shop afloat could match the Yamato in ship-to-ship action in 1942

As with other battleships of the war, the weapon's shells were so big and heavy that they could not be manned by hand by sailors. An intricate automated loading system was thus built to load them. The big ordinance came from a fortified chamber below the turret and was brought up by an elevator.

A lifting system moved the shell horizontally and pushed it into the gun magazine. Then, the automated system pressed the gunpower charges through the same process.

On that fateful March 1st, 1942, the Yamato fired in anger for the first time. Its aim was not a difficult target. It fired directly into Pearl harbor and didn't need any of the sophistication provided by its Type 92 analog targeting computer, then considered top of the line in terms of technology.

And so the guns of the great ship barked their power and unloaded their first nine 18.1-inch shells broadside at poor Oahu. The explosion created by the shells exiting the cannon's mouths was a fantastic display of fire and might. Water in front of the ship rippled, obviously raked by the Yamato's shockwave. The boat, a great behemoth of steel and weight, even rocked slightly to the right, so strong the recoil on the guns.

Sometime later, the shells landed amidst a storm of fire and anger at Pearl Harbor. Two shells created catastrophic explosions on Hickam Field, completely gutting a runway (no more flight operation would happen that day on it). Three more straddled closely to the ships in the harbor itself; two went wide and hit the side of the Oahu mountains, rocking them with an explosion worthy of a story in itself. The last two landed in a grouping of destroyers and light cruisers, creating significant damage amongst them, exploding the cruiser Aurora outright with a direct hit and damaging the rest with a shockwave and secondary explosions.

And the shelling went on for a long while; every gun that could bear in the Imperial Navy fired madly at the harbor, completely leveling everything in sight. Not one ship anchored in Pearl would actually survive the day, attacked as they were from the air and by the battleships offshore.

March 1st, 1942

Lieutenant Harry Bergman had just been able to lift, and it had been a real close call. His plane had been on the runway, almost about to liftoff from the runway, when it got hit by a tremendous explosion that rocked the world around the P-40. He barely controlled his fighter, whose rear tail was deflected by the blast.

Fortunately for Bergman, he was able to lift off, but not before the ground and air just about him got riddled with shells from a Zero fighter. It added to the airfield's tarmac's destruction and lifted up more debris in the air. But the Warhawk fighter thundered through the hailstorm unscathed. The fact that the Japanese pilot missed was a miracle, as an aircraft taking off was slow and vulnerable. Harry decided that he'd been saved by the very blast that almost killed him, throwing off the Jap's aim.

The American flyer pushed his throttle to the maximum to climb as fast as possible and get the most speed. Before waiting his turn to take off from Hickam Field, he'd seen many of his colleagues destroyed while still on the runway or else in the initial stages of climbing in the air. Jap Zero fighters hovered over the field and waited for more brave U.S. pilots to try and run the gauntlet. So speed was of the essence.

As he climbed, he looked through his fighter canopy and saw that the Zero that had riddled the ground about his Warhawk was doubling back toward him. He quickly calculated that he wouldn't have time to climb fast enough or get to a speed that would give him a chance, so he opted to level down his plane and pushed as hard as he could toward the ground again.

Fifteen seconds later, he turned between two destroyed, flaming, and smoking aircraft hangars by the airfield. The buildings had been bombed quite early in the attack and still burned fiercely, with all the planes, ammo, and gasoline inside.

He knew it was almost suicidal to fly directly between the building, where he would plunge through a firestorm. Still, the Jap had already started firing his shells, and Bergman could see the red tracers zipping by his plane, exploding just in front of him on the ground.

Harry lowered his P-40 even more to fly about five meters from the ground. And then he almost closed his eyes as he entered the raging inferno. The fire from both buildings seemed to be fused together, and the space between them was filled with fire, so he was in a red whirlpool momentarily. His aircraft nonetheless zipped past danger without a scratch, shooting out like a trailblazing star. The Japanese pilot followed closely behind. By some stroke of luck for the American, the moment the Zero fighter thundered hard between the buildings was the moment another ammunition crate exploded, sending shrapnel and other debris in the air. The Jap pilot never had a chance, and his plane exploded mid-flight.

Bergman could finally take some altitude as his pursuer was done for. By the time he climbed into the sky and above Pearl Harbor, the battle was in full fury, and his view was a scene of utter destruction. The moment he took to the sky coincided with the Japanese recall orders over the radio to fly back to the aircraft carriers for the Japs to replenish their ammo and gasoline level before coming for a fourth strike.

Some enemy aircraft were still in his immediate vision, but they all pointed eastward, probably toward their aircraft carriers. Below, it was pandemonium. From his height, Bergman was horrified at the destruction; flaming ships, burning buildings, and destroyed airfields. Even some of the water in the harbor was on fire since it had so much petrol from nearby destroyed and exploding ships floating on its surface.

He could still see Japanese shells (from surface ships) arcing over the mountains in the center of the island to land in Pearl and Honolulu, adding even more chaos and destruction to the scene. The Japanese vessels seemed to be just over the other side of the Island, on what the locals called the Winward Side. He suspected that they'd already attacked Kaneohe Base and Bellows Beach Airfield. He also noticed that not all of the Nipponese ships aimed at the harbor or the city but were dueling with the Diamond Head land fortifications.

Diamond Head was a fortress built on top of a mountain above Honolulu. The fortress's job was to defend against a ship attack, which was precisely what it was doing. But it didn't seem to be faring well. Explosions racked it constantly, and it seemed to have been heavily bombed from the air, as the mountain and surrounding jungle were on fire.

The fortification fired at the ships in defense, but their return salvos seemed insufficient to weather away the storm of shells landing on it.

It was obvious that the Americans were not winning the battle. Bergman didn't really know what to do. He was armed as a fighter and so wouldn't even scratch the paint on the battleships pounding Diamond Head. The enemy aircraft were gone, and the radio was a confused mess of people yelling and trying to get through for some reason or another. He had some time because his gas tank was full, so he decided to fly over the Japanese fleet and see if he could find some target of opportunity.

March 1st, 1942

Admiral Yamamoto could see the planes returning overhead from the third strike against Pearl Harbor and the other Oahu facilities. It had been a good day. The first three strikes had basically crippled the American fleet still anchored in the harbor. The three battleships that his planes and ships had sunk in the shallow waters were of great importance for the operation's success. According to the pilot's after-action reports, countless smaller ships like cruisers and destroyers were also sinking to the bottom or ceased to exist.

Most airfields had been heavily attacked in the first, second, and third strike, and while airplane losses had been higher than expected, the Imperial Navy was now master of the skies. He had given the order, at midday, for the battlewagons to approach the island of Oahu, to be in a position to intercept the reported ships that got out of Pearl, and also to bombard enemy ground forces position with their big guns. And so they'd shelled Pearl, and the damage report was astounding. They'd sunk several ships and finished destroying the airfields, barracks, and other defensive installations. American fire had greatly diminished.

The fleet approached the Island on the side of the prevailing winds, called the Windward Side by the locals. It was the green and lush part of Oahu, the rain mostly stopping at the mountains in the middle of the island, carried by the winds. The other side was dry and sported a lighter brown color. Yamamoto had chosen the Kaneohe military base as his first shore bombardment target. The troop landings were still a day away, the transport ships waiting, safely from a distance, for the coast to be clear. Once the base had been thoroughly flattened, they would move on to a couple of smaller military installations and then face the dreaded Diamond Head land fortifications. Those fortifications, overlooking Honolulu, could stop any landing ships on its track. It had several fixed guns of big caliber (300mm and more) that could seriously damage the Navy. He had ordered it attacked, but he was no fool in thinking that only planes would reduce this major defensive work.

As per his orders, the five battleships and five heavy cruisers opened up simultaneously, making for a fantastic display of power. The shells from the big ships took no time to travel to their destination, creating incredible destruction. The admiral could hear the resounding boom of Yamato's big cannons and the ship's small but perceptible side recoil every time the awesome weapons fired. If he concentrated, he could even see the shells arcing toward their target and exploding in a catastrophic maelstrom.

The airstrikes after-action reports had reported that the many attacks in the first wave had destroyed several U.S. ships. What was left of the American Pacific fleet in Pearl, much diminished after the transfers to the Atlantic to fight the Nazis, was utterly destroyed. The Admiral even hoped to salvage some of the units for the Imperial Navy.

So far, the oil reserve tanks and refineries near Honolulu were unscathed as per his orders (no attacks had been executed in their vicinity). Yamamoto hoped to capture them intact to replenish his fleet and operate from Oahu a lot faster than would have been possible otherwise. Japanese oil tankers would eventually have to follow up the Hawaiian offensive and ship petrol across the Pacific. So, having intact infrastructures was essential to the strategic mastermind's plans. In the meantime, he also hoped that what was in Oahu would sustain the fleet for several months if it could stay undamaged.

He turned to face a military staff member who slightly bowed to him before delivering his message: "Sir, Admiral Nagumo reports that the third wave's return and re-arming will take several hours. The first pilot landing on Akagi also said heavy American flak fire and some Yankee planes were still in the skies. "The man handed out the piece of paper containing much of the message.

The battle was not over, but he was confident that the main American Pacific base would fall to his glorious forces. "Good," he said, looking at the staff officer. "Sail the fleet to duel with Diamond Head." With that, the Japanese surface fleet began to move toward the final big battle of the invasion, the destruction of the Diamond Head fortifications.

March 1st, 1942

Lieutenant Bergman approached the Japanese fleet at full speed in a downward plunge, giving him even more momentum. The ships immediately spotted him when he appeared over the lush mountains and blanketed the sky with flak explosions, rocking the American plane and filling the sky with dark puffs of smoke. Some flak ordinances even hit the mountains, igniting fires and exploding rocks and trees off its surface.

The P-40 wasn't armed with any bombs or torpedoes, but the Japanese sailors didn't know it, so they assumed it was approaching for an attack run. Harry hadn't planned for this much of a reaction from the enemy and didn't know if he would survive his approach.

But he'd seen so much destruction that he'd be damned if he didn't at least strafe the deck of one of those big battleships busy lobbing shells at the American fortress.

The Japanese flak gunners never adjusted through Bergman's approach, and he ran the gauntlet unscathed, apart from a few bumps and scares. The giant battleship he'd targeted was growing rapidly in his view, and he figured that he wouldn't have to aim. The ship was the biggest bugger he'd seen in his life.

The flak was growing heavier by the second, and he figured that he would be shot down if he continued on the straight course he was on. He pulled his stick up and, simultaneously, blazed away with everything he had on the ship. His shells ricocheted wildly on the battleship's armor in a million sparks flying everywhere. A split second later, he flashed by the central conning tower of the ship. He continued on and planned to make a wide turn, trying again to dodge the flurry of flak explosions following him (it seemed that all the Jap ships were firing at him now).

But then he saw several black dots on the horizon far away and guessed they were enemy planes, for they came from the east, so he decided that prudence was the better part of valor. Rightly figuring out that not all the chain islands were under attack, he directed his P-40 toward the Big Island (the island called Hawaii) and planned to land there. He wasn't fleeing or being a coward; there wasn't any airfield to return to on Oahu.

Minoru Genda reports to Admiral Nagumo, March 1st, 1942

Landing on a carrier was perhaps one of aviation's most challenging feats during the Second World War. In fact, even ace pilots like Minoru Genda were more anxious about a night-time or dusk carrier landing than combat. Fortunately for him, it was the middle of the afternoon, so he would be able to land, even if there was a strong wind and the Akagi was sailing at full speed.

A carrier-based pilot had several things to consider landing his plane without incident. First, he had to do all the things a pilot landing on an airfield had to master speed, landing gears, height, length of the runway, and wind. Then, he had to consider the aircraft carrier's speed and the sea, which wasn't always calm, making for a "moving" runway. Finally, the carrier's length was never close to a land-based airfield, hence why the plane had a hook so cables placed on the carrier's deck could stop them if the pilot overshot his approach.

The mid-afternoon gale was weak, so Genda figured his landing wouldn't be difficult. It was a welcome prospect since he was already tired after three strikes on Pearl. "Commander, you are cleared for landing." It was the dry voice of the radio operator on Akagi's bridge. The plane just before he had landed, so he lined up gently right after it and eased on his throttle to slow down his aircraft. Twenty seconds later, his wheels were nicely touching the deck. His landing was so well done that he didn't even need the hook to stop his machine.

A couple of deck mechanics and signalers approached his plane and gave him the all-clear to exit. He opened his canopy and got out in a couple of swift moves. A staff officer was waiting for him at the central tower's entrance, from where he planned to get to the officer's mess to relax while his plane was re-armed and refueled.

The officer, one of Admiral Nagumo's men, bowed respectfully toward him. "Commander Genda," he started as gently as he could. "Admiral Nagumo would like to have a word with you." The officer finished by gesturing for Minoru to follow him. "Fine. Lead the way", answered the ace pilot.

He was brought to the Akagi's Bridge, where Admiral Chuichi Nagumo stood surrounded by plenty of men busy at their tasks.

On 10 April 1941, Nagumo was appointed commander-in-chief of the First Air Fleet, the IJN's main carrier battle group, primarily due to his seniority. Many in the Imperial Navy (including Genda himself) doubted his suitability for such an important command, given his lack of familiarity with naval aviation. The old admiral had already argued with Yamamoto about his doubts about the Oahu operation's potential for success. In the months leading to the attack, he'd argued about the risk and the fact that Hawaii was too far from Japan to be conquered by the Imperial forces.

More recently (on the same day of March 1942), he'd even tried to oppose Yamamoto in launching a third strike on Pearl Harbor. Minoru was sure that if Nagumo had been the only senior admiral in the theater, he would have ordered a retreat after the second strike and derailed the whole operation.

And now Genda guessed what the old man wanted to talk about. What the Akagi's air commander had in front of him was an over-the-hill naval officer, more suited for World War One-style operations. Doubts and insecurities raked the man, and it showed in every aspect of his command, down to his micro-management of all operational and tactical details that should have been left to junior officers so he could concentrate on doing an excellent job in overall command.

"Commander Genda," started Nagumo. He was dressed in the all-white of Japanese admirals, and while he looked the part, Minoru didn't have one ounce of true respect for him. "I am not certain we should send a fourth wave of attack on Pearl Harbor. The pilots are tired, and we've lost several aircraft to heavy anti-aircraft fire. What are your thoughts on this?" Several deck officers stirred uncomfortably around the admiral, trying to look the part of the busy sailor concentrating on his duties and seemingly ignoring the discussion between the two men. "With all due respect, Admiral," started the pilot, "The Americans are finished. Resistance is minimal, most of their fleet is gutted, and there is no airfield left from where to land and refuel their aircraft, let alone take off to try and battle us in the sky. So no, I don't believe a fourth wave of attack is anywhere near risky." "Well," said Nagumo hesitantly. "Thank you for your input, commander. I will contact Yamamoto about the matter. That will be all, thank you."

Genda took the message and turned around to leave. He'd been dismissed and had not given the answer the admiral hoped for. The over-cautious old man would now try to argue it over with the Grand Admiral for all the good it would do him. As he walked down the stairs back to the officer's mess, Genda didn't doubt for a second that Yamamoto would want to send a fourth strike at the enemy.

And so, for this battle, all was well since the greatest Japanese strategic mind was the overall commander, and he was within quick radio range. But Minoru thought with uneasiness, Yamamoto wouldn't always be there to impose his will on Nagumo, and the old too-cautious admiral would eventually be the senior commander.

He hoped it wouldn't be a critical battle.

Chateau Frontenac, Quebec, Late evening of March 1st, 1942

Winston Churchill continued to listen to the Chief of the Imperial General Staff, Sir Alan Brooke, reciting the latest developments in the disastrous conflict. He could not get rid of the sense of dread he was feeling. Intellectually, he knew that nothing was lost yet, and that victory was still attainable by a large margin, but reciting the news from the front was not positive.

The United Kingdom was occupied, and Allied forces were only resisted by the tiniest margins on the Agadir Front in Western Africa. The presentation was well into its second hour and was just about to end (he was looking forward to its end; he was out of cigars and scotch).

But the last part of the discussion was suddenly interrupted by a junior officer who stormed into the room, dropping in a very excited tone that Japan was attacking Pearl Harbor. The Imperial forces also invaded or attacked Hong Kong, the Malay peninsula, and Singapore.

The Japs had finally made their move. A sudden silence hung between Brooke and Churchill while the junior officer left the room, but not before dropping the full telegram report in the British Prime Minister's hand. A few short phrases described what was happening around the Pacific in the British possessions. There was a powerful land attack on Hong Kong, where a Canadian brigade reported overwhelming forces entering the city from all sectors and being bombed by numerous enemy planes. A large airstrike in the town of Singapore. Troops reported advancing in Thailand, bound for the Malay Peninsula. Several Japanese fleets were sailing toward Borneo...

Winston stopped reading. He just had enough for the day. "Alan, let's reconvene tomorrow and prepare a full report on this new development."

He stood up, seemingly shellshocked, and walked out of the office, which was, in fact, one of the hotel's suites that now served as the HQ of the British Empire.

There didn't seem to be any safe place for the English anymore. The Axis was everywhere and attacking everywhere.

Late March 1st, 1942

Roosevelt was looking at the piece of telegram in front of him on his desk. General Marshall, Admiral King, and Secretary of State Cordell Hull were with him in the room. With a large swoop of his left hand, he tossed the little piece of paper into the air. It fluttered slowly down on the floor.

For a few seconds, he stood there, looking, empty-eyed, at the ceiling. No one else dared speak in the room. The President could feel a low rumble coming from the very depths of his soul. The damned Japanese were attacking Hawaii! They had known that war was imminent with Japan ever since the oil embargo had become a reality. Hell, they had even asked for it. He'd signed the order personally...

But they never thought that the Japs would actually pull off an attack against the most heavily defended American base in the Pacific. Yes, they had sort of invited an attack by removing the most critical naval assets from the base in their war with the Third Reich. Roosevelt and King had also estimated that good old General MacArthur would have to face an invasion in the Philippines. Guam was undoubtedly going to be occupied.

But never Oahu! The radio communication from Pacific Fleet commander Admiral Kimmel was dire. The whole Pacific Fleet was either destroyed or bottled up in port. Four airstrikes had already flattened most of the defenses around Pearl Harbor, and battleships dueled with the Diamond Head fortifications. They shore-bombarded the coast at Kaneohe and Bellow's military bases. It was believed that the Jap navy would simply roll up the whole coast of the island with their big guns. The only saving grace was that most of the U.S. battleships had taken to sea before the attack on war exercises or were elsewhere in the Atlantic. So they were safe for now, along with the aircraft carriers that were also busy operating off the coast of Morocco.

There were no signs of ground troops yet. Still, King and Marshall believed that if the Japanese battlewagons were present in the numbers suggested by Kimmel and that they were shore-bombarding military and ground installations, Nipponese troops would be close behind the attack.

"Send for the relevant people," he said in a low voice. "I have an address to Congress to prepare," he said slowly. "George, well, make them pay. Damn, I am mad!" the President finished with his fist in the air.

When America woke up the next day, it discovered the extent of Japanese treachery and the magnitude of the developing military disaster. The Oahu attack also seriously derailed the carefully discussed plans with the rest of the Allies, done only weeks before at a strategy conference.

As President Roosevelt would adeptly say in his March 2nd, 1942, address to Congress, March 1st, 1942, would live as a day in infamy. War raged across the Pacific, from Hong Kong, the American Philippines, Singapore, Borneo, and Sumatra. The Japanese Empire's tide was overwhelming, and it seemed they attacked everywhere at once.

March 2nd, 1942

Lieutenant Takashi Onishi slowly lifted off the runway with his Zero fighter, pulling with skills on his flight stick in his right hand and putting more power to the throttle with his left hand. The ground started to blur as the aircraft picked up speed, and the Japanese pilot took to the air.

It didn't take long for the radio to give him his orders. "All pilots, assemble." Onishi was one of the last men to takeoff from the airfield for the first strike on the Philippines. "We're heading for Clark Field. Banzai!" And then voices repeated their wing commander's last word in the typical enthusiasm of the Imperial Navy pilots.

As his plane leveled into formation and took its place in the V-shaped arrangement that would bring them over to the Philippines, Onishi tried to take in the immensity of the moment.

He was a young but somewhat experienced pilot in the Imperial Navy. He'd fought many dogfights in China over Hankow, the Nationalist Chinese capital city, in 1937 before the Army conquered it. As such, he'd been able to have some valuable fighting experience that would come in handy in the war that was just starting.

Onishi was already considered an ace, with five victories to his total at the start of World War Two. He was the product of a very selective training program. Japan made things quite difficult for pilots in the Navy, and only the best of the best made it to pilot status. Every year, over 5000 applicants from all over the fleet tried to get into the pilot flight school (Kasumigaura Airfield), and out of that, around 65 were selected, and the rigidity and difficulty of the training course flunked about fifty per year. So, only twenty-five to forty pilots emerged annually within the Japanese Army ranks. It gave them elite status from the start, as they had the

best reflexes, the best scores, and the best of everything.

While the system produced top-echelon pilots like Onishi, it wasn't made for wartime and its realities, where casualties and normal attrition dwindled numbers down to a mere trickle without replacements. But that was in the future, and now, Japan boasted the best flyers in the world, and for a while, they would give their enemy hell.

Takashi took the time to look around his plane's canopy. There were several V-shaped formations flying side by side. Bombers were also there, represented by the excellent Mitsubishi G3M and Mitsubishi G4M bombers. The fifty or so of them each carried 130 lb. of bomb ordinance in their bellies. Onishi and his other fighter comrades' job was to protect the slower aircraft so they could drop their bombs and then find and destroy the enemy on the ground.

The flight took several hours, during which not much happened, and total radio silence was maintained. So, it was somewhat dull for the pilots, but at the same time, most were jittery with nervousness and anticipation. Takashi knew he would be soaked in sweat again after the battle. It was just the way it was. Aerial dogfight and airstrike missions took everything a pilot had regarding energy, concentration, and resourcefulness.

The first wave of Japanese bombers (which Onishi was part of) approached by early afternoon. By the time U.S. airmen in Clark Field realized they were under attack, the bombs were already falling down on their heads.

A few gun crews got their antiaircraft weapons working during the Japanese attack but weren't very effective due to several faulty shells that never exploded.

Takashi looked down after his first attack run, where he'd strafed a line of Brewster Buffalo fighters, and saw some sixty enemy bombers and fighters neatly parked along the airfield runways a bit further down by a large hangar. The Americans seemingly had made no attempt to disperse the planes and increase their safety. So, he pushed his throttle to maximum, followed by several of his comrades, and again hit the fire button, releasing a wave of 20mm shells from his Type 99 cannon at the enemy aircraft. His wingmates did the same, and they were all rewarded with several crafts exploding and more receiving hits, shattering them apart and making thousands of debris pieces fly into the air. Takashi was even worried for a moment when he crossed a blossoming cloud of smoke skyrocketing into the air after the plane that had produced it had been hit by the Jap pilot's ordinance. Such was the "risk of flying low over a target you tried to destroy" as one of his instructors at the flight academy had repeatedly battered their heads. But he was lucky this time, and apart from some shaking, his Zero fighter was unscathed.

Bombs crashed into barracks and service buildings around the Japanese planes preying on Clark Airfield. Much of the airplane maintenance equipment was destroyed, going up into flame, and with it, the entire American radar installation.

For a moment, Onishi felt elated since the battle was so one-sided it seemed to be like his early training days where they were shooting at stationary targets, or even his time in China, where the Nationalist forces didn't have much to oppose them in the air. But unbeknownst to the Japanese pilot, a few American P-40 fighters were able to lift up during the attack, dodging the maelstrom and evading destruction by some sheer stroke of luck.

The aircraft was one of the US's most recent airplanes but was outclassed by the Japanese Zero's superior speed and maneuverability. Nonetheless, a couple of American pilots shot down two Jap fighters before the attackers realized some enemies were in the air. Onishi quickly veered his plane up, pushing his throttle to maximum and pulling hard on his flying stick to gain altitude. When he felt he'd taken enough elevation, he'd already spotted a P-40 chasing one of his comrades, blazing away with its ammo, red tracers zipping by the beleaguered Nipponese plane. He plunged again in a semi-loop and, within seconds, fired away again with his 20mm cannon, riddling the American aircraft with shells and shredding it catastrophically. The enemy disintegrated in midair, and its flaming debris showered an already raging inferno below on stricken Clark Field.

Six more waves would hit the Philippines' many airbases that day, and more would be launched by the Imperial Navy and Army before the ordeal was over. By the time the Jap forces approached the Lingayen Gulf beaches a few days later, the U.S. air force had nothing to send against them.

March 3rd, 1942

Imperial Navy landing doctrine was becoming a finely-honed art for the Japanese since they had been perfecting them in the conflict with China. The fact that the Nipponese military prepared for a war of conquest across the Pacific theater also compounded both the Navy and Army to work on solutions and developments of tactics and equipment to make this work.

For one, most Japanese attacks were usually conducted at night and thus unopposed most of the time. In some instances, when a landing did come under fire, the boats transporting the men would move to a new site. Reconnaissance of amphibious-suited areas was performed by air or sea, with boots on the ground rarely landing ahead of time.

In the case of the Hawaii attack, the Americans received such a pounding for three days that Yamamoto decided to land all of his forces in a couple of extensive grouped operations near Waikiki Beach (near Honolulu) and at Bellows Beach on the Winward Side. Both places were suitable for such operations, as the water had shallow depths, and the beaches were long and large.

There was no real opposition when the first Japanese soldier set foot in the water by Honolulu since the Diamond Head fortifications had been silenced the day before. American troops (brigade-sized force after the other soldiers had left for the Atlantic in 1941) had fled to the mountains in the middle of the island, where their chances of survival, which were already pretty slim, were greater than staying on the open to face the guns of the Japanese battleships Nagumo's aircraft carriers.

The fierce-looking Imperial troops advanced with grim determination, and not even a civilian came to see what they were doing. The city of Honolulu was mainly leveled, and the survivors were hiding.

The 123rd Imperial Regiment encountered some resistance near Kaneohe, where a local grouping of surviving U.S. soldiers put up a bit of a fight. Still, in the end, it was quickly overwhelmed.

In total, the Japanese landed three divisions in Hawaii in the first five days of the attack, so by the 5th of March, they had most of Oahu firmly under control. Some of the American G.I.s resisted a bit more (for a couple of weeks) in the deep jungles of the mountains in the center of the island, but they soon surrendered, out of ammunition and food.

By the 5th, the Imperial flag towered above Diamond Head, and the Island of Oahu was considered secure. Yamamoto then ordered troops to be sent to the other islands, and within another week, Molokai, Kauai, Maui, and Lanai were occupied. On the 13th, a more extensive operation was executed against the Big Island (Hawaii), but again the scarcity of American troops didn't make resistance last very long.

On the 15th of March, Grand Admiral Yamamoto cabled to Tokyo that the Hawaiian Islands were under complete Japanese control and called for the reinforcements he'd planned. Another four divisions would be moved to the Island Chain, along with over 500 fighters, 300 fighter-bombers, and plenty of Imperial engineers/slave workers to build airfields and prepare the fortifications to help keep Pearl Harbor for the duration.

March 12th, 1942

As he climbed down the small steel ladder of the USS Nautilus hatch (a Narwhal-class submarine for the U.S. Navy), Lieutenant Harry Bergman could not help but feel a little shame. He was escaping, fleeing in the face of the enemy.

Intellectually, he knew it wasn't a choice but a necessity. Staying would have either amounted to his death (if he'd flown in his P-40) or imprisonment (if he got captured by the soon-to-land Japanese forces).

As water fell on his head from the hatch closing above, he dropped to the main submarine room, hitting the steel deck with a metalling clang. Most of the submariners looked at him with smiles on their faces. "Welcome, lieutenant," said Lieutenant Commander William H. Brockman Jr., the Sub's commanding officer. A loud bang was heard above. The hatch was closed shut.

"Sail and Dive," was the first officer's order, busy manning the sub while his Brockman Jr. talked to Bergman. "Thank you, lieutenant commander," answered Harry respectfully. "Please follow this man; he will show you to your accommodations," finished the submariner leader, pointing to a midshipman. "I'll join you for a chat later."

The USS Nautilus was about to dive and was busy ensuring they could escape the Japanese unscathed. Four more boats were leaving the Big Island on the same day because of the Nipponese attack. The Island had been raided for days, and everything in sight had been leveled. They'd discussed fighting, but the joint decision had been to return to the mainland. The U.S. Navy had been broadcasting for all units near the Hawaiian Islands to gather back to the harbors on the Californian coast.

Bergman had been included in the minimal spaces that the Nautilus had because he was a pilot. They didn't bring any civilians, just men who could help with the war effort, like pilots and engineers.

As he walked the tight confines of the submarine, Harry tried to look back at the last two weeks. First, he'd fought over Hawaii and then had flown to the Big Island in desperation, making it barely for lack of fuel. He'd flown several more sorties until it became apparent that going into the air again was tantamount to suicide because the Japanese forces were heavily patrolling the sky above Kona. So, on the 10th, he'd put his plane to the torch and joined the submariners for the trip back to America.

Bergman didn't consider himself a stubborn man, but after what the Japs had done to his country, he'd be damned if he didn't come back on a plane to fight them off Hawaii and beyond.

The start of the conflagration

I was notified very late on March 1st about the Japanese attack on Pearl Harbor without receiving any details about the outcome of the battle. It was our strongest military position in the Pacific, albeit slightly weakened by the recent force removal and transfers to the Atlantic theater. The island had a very strong garrison and a truly powerful fort (Fort Ruger inside Diamond Head). Furthermore, Oahu had a lot of fighters and bombers, including anti-aircraft defenses, radar, and all of that, protected by the still-powerful Pacific Fleet. Finally, the distance involved in a potential Japanese attack was so great that my imagination didn't even consider the possibility of a Japanese attack or an invasion. My only thoughts when I hung up the phone were that the Japanese had been severely defeated and that we were still in control of the situation. It is difficult to fathom our wrong I was in my assessment.

Contrary to my belief, we had just been handed out the worst defeat in all of American history. The Japanese succeeded in attacking Oahu and demolished everything of value on the Islands. There were even talks of Japanese landings. Battleships were sunk, and American defenses were destroyed. It was an utter shock to everyone in my command, including myself.

We never thought the Japanese were capable of defeating the USA on such a scale. The whole affair gave us all a sense of foreboding about the future. On the first and second of March, several heavy airstrikes were conducted against our forces in Clark Airfield and other bases. Obviously, our enemy enjoyed a comfortable superiority in terms of the number of planes.

Reports came in from everywhere in the Pacific about Japanese attacks: Guam was bombarded by ships and planes, and some troop ships were sighted. A British heavy cruiser had been sunk off the coast of Malaya. Singapore was being bombed hourly. Hong Kong was already amid a serious battle between Canadian forces and numerous Imperial Army troops. More airstrikes in the Dutch East Indies and reported landing in Sumatra.

It was not pretty, and I wondered if we could stem the yellow tide threatening to engulf us all during those first few dark days of the war.

CHAPTER 2

The Battle of Hong Kong

Canada's struggle in the Far East, March 2nd to March 25th

War for Canada arrived at the same time as the rest of the British Empire in September 1939, but its army saw little action since the start of the conflict. The population and its leaders were a little hesitant to commit troops as the memory of the Great War's bloodbath was still fresh in everyone's mind.

However, after the Wehrmacht occupation of the United Kingdom, public opinion and Canada's stance toward the war changed. First and foremost, the British government in exile, with Churchill at its head, moved to French Canada, headquartering itself in the Chateau Frontenac in Quebec City. This act alone put Canada at the forefront of the Second World War as the seat of the British Empire. French and English Canadians alike suddenly supported the war entirely, as everyone saw the dangers of letting the Nazis win in Europe. If nothing was done, they would eventually come to North America. Besides, the US was also in the fight, which was enough for the brave Canadians.

Canadian destroyers from the RCN (Royal Canadian Navy) were already involved in convoy protection, while some pilots had crossed over during the Battle of Britain and the subsequent invasion of the Germans, but the ground troops had not yet been called upon. With the worsening of relations with Japan and the increasing shortage of soldiers, the British found themselves in compounded Churchill to request the Canadian government (Prime Minister Mckenzie King) to help with troops in Asia, and more specifically for the protection of the Hong Kong colony on the Chinese mainland.

The Japanese Empire had been waging war in China since 1937, but

it had avoided open hostilities against the West. By 1941, the British were fighting for survival against Germany. They realized that defending Hong Kong would be virtually impossible if the colony and other Asian possessions were attacked by Japan. Even so, Britain decided that a show of force might deter any possible Japanese aggression, and it sought troops to reinforce the British and Indian units already garrisoned in Hong Kong. The Canadian Army thus allotted two brigades for the mission and sailed them to Hong Kong at the end of 1940.

On March 1st, 1942 — almost four months after the Canadians arrived in Hong Kong and settled into the quiet routines of garrison life — Japan took its fateful plunge toward destiny and attacked the United States naval fleet at Pearl Harbor, Hawaii. It also launched an offensive against the British, Dutch, French, and Australian forces arrayed against them. Suddenly, the whole Pacific theatre was aflame, and a city like Hong Kong was at the top of the Japanese hitlist. Some defenses had been prepared, but not as much as they should have been. The very nature of what they were defending – a city – didn't allow the Canadians to set up trenches and other logical wartime preparations.

Not even half a day following the Pearl Harbor attack and amphibious invasion, the Japanese attacked Hong Kong with the 38th Imperial Infantry Division. The unit was an elite formation with years of fighting experience in China and top-of-the-line equipment. The Japanese started by bombing out the city, the harbor, and the known defensive positions, followed by an all-out Assault with their infantry forces.

The fight that ensued would last a little over three weeks, but the conclusion was already known from the start. While the Canadian troops fought well and with courage, there was no hope for them as they were isolated in the middle of the Japanese Empire, with no hope of resupply or reinforcement. The beleaguered Allies were on the retreat everywhere and being defeated at every turn across the entire Pacific. Thus, the plight of the two poor Canadian brigades went unanswered.

But they did fight like demons and forced the hand of the Japanese Army command in China, who had to send reinforcements to break them (the 45th Imperial Division) from its China campaign in order to help with the final assault on Hong Kong Island. A heavy cruiser (the Kinugasa with its 155mm naval guns) was also called to help shore-bombard the desperate defenders.

The Allied forces in Hong Kong finally surrendered on March 25th, 1942, after almost a month of grueling battle and death. The fighting utterly demolished the city, and civilian casualties climbed well over 300,000. Of the original Canadian 14,000 soldiers that began the defense of Hong Kong, only 8,000 were taken prisoner. The harsh treatment of soldiers by the Japanese killed another 2,500, so only 1,500 would survive the war to go home to their loved ones.

The Japanese attack through March 1942

Under Admiral Yamamoto's and Hajime's plan, the Japanese wanted to occupy the Philippines because it was a steppingstone for the south, where the real prizes lay for Japan. With the Philippine's, it was then possible to conquer the resources the Empire needed for its continued expansion and military forces in Southeast Asia (Dutch East Indies, Malaya, and the like). At the same time (as part of the grand plan), the Imperial Navy was to neutralize the United States Pacific Fleet and occupy key islands in the Pacific. The Philippines was central to Japanese strategic thinking since it lay between southeast Asian resources and the Japanese factories in the Home Islands. The shipping sea lanes would pass right by them, and the American military presence in the Philippines could not be ignored.

The invasion of the Philippines had two critical objectives. First, it was to prevent American forces from using the Philippines as an advanced base of operations. Then, Japan needed to acquire staging areas and supply bases to enhance operations against the Dutch East Indies and Guam. As said earlier, it was about securing the lines of communication between the planned conquests in the south.

General Masaharu Homma (Japanese 14th Army) was entrusted with the execution of the invasion. All of the air assets to support the invasion were stationed in Peleliu and Formosa (5th Imperial Air Force)

During the preparation for the Pacific War, the Japanese Army transferred a lot of troops from its Kwantung Army, which was guarding the border with the Soviet Union and also warring against the Nationalist Chinese and warlords in Northern China. Russia and Japan had been in a constant unofficial state of war since the incident in 1939 across the borders of Siberia. At the same time, the Russians had their hands full with the war in Europe. The war against the Chinese had been raging since 1937. The Sino forces were on the defensive only, lacking the means to attack since they mostly lacked artillery tanks and, most importantly, planes. So, it was deemed an acceptable risk to use the troops elsewhere for the conquest of the resources the Empire needed so badly. The trend would continue throughout the Pacific War as Japan's fortunes dropped steadily against the Allies.

The battle opened with a fury a couple of hours after the first shot was fired in anger in Peal Harbor, with a powerful Japanese airstrike on Clark Airfield, where the Japanese air units caught many American planes still on the ground. General Bereton, the commander of the US Air Force in Luzon, had some forces over the area in combat air patrol (CAP), but they got overwhelmed since they were outnumbered ten to one. Most of the bomber squadron based in the Philippines (fifty B-17s) were destroyed on the ground, as the American leadership still debated if they should organize a strike on Formosa.

The land invasion followed soon after, and by the 8th of March, the Imperial forces (14th Army) had destroyed the two Filipino divisions defending Northern Luzon. General Homma thus ordered his forces to advance inland to destroy the Allied forces near the Filipino capital and Clark Airfield near it.

In the south, Mindanao was also invaded as planned. The Nipponese forces made landfall on the 9th of March. They made their way rapidly inland since there weren't many American or Filipino units to defend the large island. By the 11th, it was all over, and Davao, the area's main city, was in Japanese hands. Some pockets of resistance stayed alive and were left alone by the Japs, which had more important objectives southward than storm jungle strongholds.

Extract of Tameichi Hara's book Teikoku Kaigun no Saigo 1967

The Davao Operation, March 3rd, 1942

After the combined fleet gathering in Hiroshima Bay, my destroyer Amatsukaze was ordered to Peleliu, the main harbor on the island of Palau. We were part of a powerful task force built around the small aircraft carrier Ryujo. The remaining naval group comprised the old battleship Haruna, the light cruiser Jintsu, five destroyers (Amatsukaze, Hayashio, Natsushio, Kurushio Oyashio), and several large troop transports. Our mission: land in Davao and take over the main military installation of Mindanao. Along the way, we were also powerful enough to destroy the reported American naval presence there: a Bristol-Class seaplane tender and a destroyer.

The voyage to Peleliu Harbor in Palau was without incident, and by the 18th of January, we were on the island. The following few weeks were quite good to me and the crew as we were able to train, go on maneuvers and rest on the lovely tropical paradise that was Palau Island.

All the while, relations between Japan and the Allies worsened by the day. We eventually got the order we all dreaded receiving. The historic February 27th message from Combined Fleet headquarters read, "Climb Mt. Niitaka" (the name of the highest mountain in Formosa). I gulped at this message and felt its significance even before opening the sealed secret cipher book. The words meant: "Start war against the Allies on Match 2nd, 1942."

Shortly afterward, all ship captains were gathered around rear admiral Raizo Ishaka for instruction on an attack on Davao. We were to proceed with all haste on the 2nd or 3rd (depending on local circumstances that would be left to Ishaka) and escort the large grouping of troops transports carrying the soldiers of the 23rd Army to land on Mindanao. After the conquest of Davao, we were to receive further instructions on the Borneo, New Guinea, and Celebes attacks that were also planned.

We sailed all day and night without incident, apart from a few false sonar detections. At daybreak on the 3rd, twenty light bombers and fighters were launched from Ryujo.

By mid-morning, Ryujo's planes returned, and we then learned that the aircraft had not even shot one shell in anger or dropped any bombs since they hadn't been fired at, and the reported ships were gone, with no traces of them.

By the end of the afternoon on the third, our ship and the rest of the fleet entered the quiet of Davao Bay without being challenged by either plane, ship, or radio. Along with our destroyers and the cruiser Jintsu, the transport ships moved slowly into the port, which appeared quiet and peaceful. By the time the first soldiers of the 23rd Army streamed out on the pier and into the harbor proper, some Allied troops appeared and started to fire on them.

I ordered our port guns to open fire. Our six 120mm guns rotated and fired. The docks erupted in fire and clouded in a large cloud of billowing smoke and fire, killing most of the attackers. My men continued to pour fire into the pier just to make sure and hit a large oil tank. The resulting explosion vaporized the buildings around and ensured that all of the enemies coming toward us were killed. It was the last we saw of any enemy resistance in Davao and, consequently, the only exciting action of the whole operation.

Reports later mentioned that American presence on the whole island was very light (only regimental-sized). Allied commanders had decided to move them further north where they could defend better (in the jungles of the Mindanao interior).

And thus ended our first mission of the Second World War. I was slightly disappointed by the lack of action but should have known better. It is always good to win easily in war, for when it is difficult, people die, and ships get sunk.

The Kota Bharu landings, March 2nd to 10th, 1942

Japan's invasion of Malaya, a British colony, began on the 2nd of March 1942, a few hours before the attack on Pearl Harbor. It was officially the start of the Pacific War, and the attack on Pearl Harbor is generally considered to have been where the first shots were fired in anger.

The Japanese launched the offensive with two amphibious landings. The first was in Northern Malaya (18th Division) in a town called Kota Bharu. The second landing was on Thailand's east coast (north of Khota Baru) by the 5th Imperial Division. The overall plan was for the 5th to attack and push westward and invade Malaya's West Coast and then make its way south toward Singapore, while the 18th was to push down the east coast and also toward Singapore.

The British plan to defend the Kota Bharu area included the use of fixed beach positions by the Indian 9th Infantry Division and the Australian 8th Division to defend the remainder of the coastline. While the Indians got their hands full right at the start with the Japanese landing into their midst, the Australians remained relatively unscathed in the first few days of the struggle, with no Japanese land attacks apart from some air raids.

The Imperial forces opened up the attack with a landing supported by shore bombardment attacks and several powerful air strikes from Indochina airfields. The rough conditions (the sea was very choppy during the initial phase of the landings) hampered the attack, and important losses were reported because of the amphibious boat sinking and capsizing. Despite these minor setbacks, by early morning (still in the dark of night), the first wave of the landing craft hit Bachok beach in front of Kota Bharu.

On seeing the Japanese landing craft approaching, the defending 9th

Infantry Division opened up with everything it had on the oncoming enemy. They had several excellent guns, good bunkers, and well-prepared positions overlooking the landing zones.

Finally hitting the beach after losing several ships due to the gun's heavy fire, the Japanese soldiers fought their way across the sandy ground with some difficulty and very high casualties. Still, the brave imperial troops kept trying, and after several suicidal charges followed by vicious hand-to-hand fighting, a breach was made in the Allied defenses. The whole position unraveled for the Indian unit defending the beach and city. As said earlier, Japanese casualties in the first and second waves were heavy but expected. After all, it wasn't like the imperial high command counted the dead in the Japanese Army.

It also didn't take long for the small but powerful Japanese battlefleet offshore to silence the guns pounding their IJA (Army) comrades. They picked off the Indian soldiers off the coast with heavy cruiser Myoko heavy weapons and from several light cruisers and destroyers. Their red tracer shells fired from offshore plunged into their enemy's positions and exploded the pillboxes and other defenses. The firefight lit the darkness, so the beach and surrounding areas burned for the rest of the night, illuminating the sky for the Japanese forces to continue their landing unscathed.

The very next day (at first light), General Yamashita, the commander-in-chief of all imperial forces for the Malaya campaign, splashed both feet in the water, landing amongst the elite men of his beloved 18th Division. After quickly assessing the situation, he ordered his soldiers to push inland and take the city.

News from the north was also dire for the Allies, as the 14th Infantry division's landings were also a success, and the troops were already reporting heading inland.

By the end of the 3rd of March, the battle for the city proper was over, and the 5th Imperial Division reached the west coast of Thailand and touched the Indian Ocean. Several of its forces also moved south to reinforce the 18th Division in the battle against the Indian 9th Division.

Heavy fighting continued for the best part of another week. The Allies sent more troops to the battle (the New Zealand 3rd and two more Indian divisions). The fight stayed inconclusive until the rest of Yamashita's 25th Army's forces, moving down from Thailand unopposed, approached the frontline.

By then, the British commander in Singapore (Arthur Percival), responsible for the overall command of all Allied forces in the Malay Peninsula, ordered the retreat toward Singapore and the safety of its defenses.

The destruction of Force Z, March 3rd, 1942

Two great ships plowed the waves off Malaya's northern coast on that second of March 1942. Their mission: intercept the Japanese landings and destroy the transport ships.

The County-Class heavy cruisers of the British Royal Navy were some of the best cruiser classes of World War Two. It comprised twelve ships in two other sub-classes. They sported 8-inch guns like the Japanese heavy cruisers and were also as fast as their Imperial Navy counterparts. They weren't battleships but could measure up to any other types of vessels afloat from the World's navies. And bunched up together, they could even take on a bigger ship, as was shown in the European theater of war.

The twin heavy cruisers Dorsetshire and Cornwall started the war in the Atlantic. They participated in several convoy duties and even fought the Germans in the Battle of the Channel in 1940, which saw the Wehrmacht cross and conquer the United Kingdom. The two cruisers fought gallantly against hundreds of planes. In the end, the Home Fleet was recalled north for fear of having it destroyed by the Luftwaffe. There just hadn't been enough planes to protect them.

Having been damaged in the battle, they limped back to Scapa flow and eventually made it to Halifax in Canada, where they were put in drydocks to repair the torpedo and bomb damage. The Cornwall even had one of its triple 8-inch turrets redone completely.

By April 1941, their repairs were finished, so they were ordered to the Pacific Theater. They first ran some escort duties for war supplies to Australia (with even a stop in American Samoa) and then made their way to Singapore via the Dutch East Indies.

Together, they formed the task force called "Force Z" and represented the fast-action ships for the British if war broke out. It wasn't believed that the Japanese would become a problem. For if there was to be war, western prejudices thought they would easily beat the Asian sailors and that their potential enemies had sub-par equipment and ships.

In any case, that theory was about to be put to the test, as Force Z was ordered to sortie to intercept the Japanese landings in Kota Bharu. On the third, the two vessels sped forth from the protected harbor by midday under a magnificent sun and clear skies. The sailors and officers alike thought it a good omen, for they would have excellent visibility and be able to shoot from a great distance. They couldn't have been more wrong in their happiness, for the opposite was also true. Aircraft would spot them from far away, with their silhouettes and smoke columns rising.

A small force of ten Brewster Buffalo fighters from the Australian Air Force was also called for air coverage, as it was believed that the Japanese might attempt to attack the ships while they transited to their targets.

But most within the British high command in Singapore weren't overly worried about the Japanese or that their two heavy cruisers would sail pretty much unprotected from above. The fighters were on call, meaning they weren't asked to fly over the ships at all times, but it was believed that they would be flown forth if any problem arose. After all, the Kota Bharu and Medang airfields were very close.

And so it was that the two magnificent British ships of war sailed brazenly toward their destiny. At 15h00 during that afternoon, they were spotted by a Japanese recon plane. The Mitsubishi Ki-46 was a twin-engine reconnaissance aircraft the Imperial Japanese Army used. It had an endurance of over six hours so that it could fly over the South China Sea for a long time. From the high altitude it cruised at, it was quickly able to spot the funnel smoke of the English vessels and called the main Army airfield. Ten minutes later, a large airstrike was approaching Dorsetshire and Cornwall. It was carried out by twenty-five Mitsubishi G3M "Nell' twin-engine medium bombers. They were each armed with the excellent type-94 torpedoes that were so effective in Pearl Harbor just a few days before. The aircraft was a dual-purpose machine of war and could carry bombs or torpedoes.

After an hour's flight, they finally connected with the two British ships, directed as they were by the recon plane flying high above Force Z. The British spotter didn't take long to identify an enemy airstrike, and the gun servants ran to their station. The two ships didn't have sufficient anti-aircraft defenses, as did most of the vessels in 1942, prior to the clear demonstration that planes and aircraft carriers now ruled the waves.

As the Japanese planes dove into preparing their run at the cruisers, the flak opened up on them, blanketing the sky with explosions that seemed to follow the plane's movements. In World War Two, hitting a moving aircraft was a difficult feat; with no help from radar or any other technology, one only had to rely on training, experience, and the gunner's skills.

The Dorsetshire and Cornwall blazed away at their enemies, downing two Nell bombers before they could release their torpedoes. The two ships crashed hard into the waves, exploding on impact with the sea.

But the rest, a staggering twenty-three of them, loosened their torpedoes at the beleaguered ships that zigzagged back and forth to try to present the most challenging target and avoid the enemies' ordinance.

Cornwall was the first to be hit, as it was sailing to the right of Dorsetshire, so it acted as a shield. Several Jap torpedoes missed, but three struck the ship on its starboard side, exploding catastrophically. The ship seemingly lifted up out of the water, opening in two from the middle. It spurted fire for a fleeting moment before being obliterated from existence, showering the South China Sea with flaming, smoking debris.

Dorsetshire didn't even have time to ponder its sistership's destruction as four torpedoes hit it on the starboard side. One destroyed the rudder and a good part of the ship's rear, one stuck the bow, opening it to gushing water, and two hit down the middle. One hit the ammunition magazine, creating a plume of smoke and fire that rose hundreds of feet into the air.

The second cruiser didn't explode like the first, but it sank within ten minutes, leaving a large patch of oily blackness and struggling sailors, desperate to survive the churning waters, burning oil and pieces of debris milling about.

The affair was a stark reminder for the Allies that the Japanese meant business and that they packed a serious punch. It had nothing to do with Asian or white men. It was just plain old military might.

Along with the events in Pearl Harbor (carrier planes destroying a fleet and a harbor), it clearly marked the end of the road for unescorted surface ships, regardless of how powerful they were.

Imperial Army 18th Division, March 11th, 1942

Face first in a pool of blood, private Ishiro Tanaka of the 18th Imperial Army Division looked right back at the face of the dead man beside him. The Allied soldier had his eyes open and seemed to look back directly at him.

The blood on the Japanese soldier's face came from the large gash on the Indian's belly. The man's white turban was also red with blood. Ishiro wasn't certain he'd been the one that killed him. However, it didn't matter. He picked up his Arisaka rifle that he'd let go of when he tripped and lifted himself up to start running again, yelling all the while, weapon in both hands, with a bristling bayonet on it.

He was in a non-descript farmer's field somewhere south of Kota Bharu. The 18th division (he was part of one of its component units, the 11th Regiment) had been ordered in a headlong charge against the last remnants of Allied defenders that were trying to retreat. He stopped for a second to aim his rifle. He'd spotted another enemy running, so he fired at the man's back. His weapon recoiled hard on his shoulder, and its bullet hit the mark. The retreating enemy soldier somersaulted awkwardly on the left, fell on the ground like a broken puppet, and stayed still, dead or severely injured.

Satisfied, Tanaka started running again and continued his headlong charge with his comrades toward the by-now panicked Indians. Everyone around him yelled the characteristic "Banzai!" yell that was always part of any Japanese infantry charges.

He came up to the Allied trench, now utterly devoid of any living soldiers. He sprinted a bit harder and jumped over it. The officers, Samurai sword in hand, continued to urge them forward, and they all did.

After another ten minutes, they finally got onto a large road. By then, the whole Regiment was panting hard, and everyone had stopped running because the Allied soldiers had also stopped. Ishiro wondered why for a moment but then saw a Japanese Army flag right in the path of the retreating troops. The enemy had been flanked and was now cornered. They simply lifted their arms in the air and surrendered their weapons.

Little did they know that the victorious Japanese were not lenient men. In fact, nothing was worse in Nipponese culture than surrendering to an enemy. It represented a level of shame that could not be endured. And so the officers of the 11th Regiment gestured their men forward, and everyone, including Ishiro, went into a killing frenzy and filleted every one of the defenseless soldiers in front of them. It was nothing short of a massacre, but the proud men of the 18th Division did not even ponder for half a second about what they were doing.

Ishiro Tanaka, an imperial soldier, was the embodiment of the World War Two Japanese fighting men. He felt no compassion for his enemies and was wholly dedicated to the Japanese cause, which he considered just and proper. Japan's destiny was to conquer the whole Pacific. It was the country's divine right.

And so, while he killed the helpless Indian soldiers begging to be spared, he did it with a relish (and a primal need) worthy of a serial killer.

March 8 to 18th, 1942

After successful Imperial Army landings in Lingayen Gulf and several inconclusive counterattacks by American forces, the bulk of the Japanese soldiers landed on Luzon. The Air Force and the US Navy didn't do much to oppose the landings. They were ordered to retire southward toward Australia or were already destroyed by the heavy Nipponese airstrikes of the week before. Macarthur was thus left to his own devices with his men and the Filipino forces.

The main Japanese attack began after their successful amphibious operations early on the morning of March 8, 1942. 33 110 men of the 16th, 47th, and 48th divisions supported by the tanks units pushed toward the interior, Manilla, and the Clark airfield complex.

American General Wainwright's (within Macarthur's command) poorly trained and equipped 11th Division and 71st Division did not repel the landings a few days earlier nor stopped the enemy from advancing, as the IJA (Imperial Japanese Army) was supported by naval gunfire and total air superiority. And so the Americano-Philippine forces retreated southward, fighting a delaying action. Several pockets of Allied forces got stranded or encircled by the overwhelming Japanese elsewhere across the island. They would still fight but were already doomed to surrender at one point.

The Japanese also executed more landings in the Lingayen Gulf, and the fighting quickly pushed the Allies back further inland and southward. The Americans and their Filipino comrades were completely overmatched by the imperial air superiority, naval supremacy, and overall better-trained Nipponese troops.

It didn't take an extended analysis for a man like Macarthur to see that he was severely disadvantaged. Without any hopes of being reinforced (the USA had been basically thrown out of the Pacific theater with the Pearl Harbor disaster), he quickly surmised that the situation was desperate. With no air units to counter the countless Japanese aircraft or a fleet to battle the numerous surface units pounding his men in the open or landing wherever they chose, he decided to follow up on a plan to resist as long as possible by retreating in the southern-most peninsula of the Island, where he would be able to entrench and fortify his position.

With this move, he hoped it would give time for the Allies to come to his help. On March 14th, MacArthur invoked the prewar plan WPO-3 (War Plan Orange 3), which called for a withdrawal into Bataan. He used the previous ten days to send supplies into the peninsula feverishly, primarily by barge from Manila, in an attempt to feed an anticipated force of 43,000 troops for six months. Ultimately, 80,000 troops and 26,000 refugees flooded Bataan before the final forces streamed into the area. On March 16th, MacArthur declared Manila an open city as the Japanese approached (they were mere hours from the city's outskirts).

The Japanese, thinking they'd already won the battle for Luzon, saw what the American commander wanted to do by March 16th, and General Homma pushed the 48th and 16th imperial to try and seal off the Peninsula and block more enemy troops from retreating there.

Following a series of sharp battles on the 17th and 18th, a hodgepodge of Americano-Filipino units fought hard and desperately to hold off the

Japanese attacks and to keep the road open at the neck of the Bataan Peninsula for the rest of MacArthur's units to retreat to the relative safety fortified Allied enclave. They succeeded in their attempt, losing over half of their numbers in the process. And then they retreated into Bataan. The Battle for Luzon was over, and the siege of the peninsula began.

Extract from General Macarthur's book, Reminiscences, 1964

The lead-up to Bataan, March 6th to 18th, 1942

The battle for Lingayen Gulf raged for a few days, and the 11th and 21st Divisions of the Philippine Army were soundly defeated by the superior Japanese forces, supported by their aircraft and ships. I did send some reinforcements early into this struggle. Still, with the enemy's overwhelming air and naval superiority, I quickly realized that moving troops and attacking in a too-forward way would prove detrimental to our cause.

After pushing back and defeating the 11th and 21st Filipinos, the enemy advanced inland surprisingly fast for an un-mechanized army. The Nipponese proved quite mobile even in jungle terrain. They were well-trained and well-equipped with thousands of bicycles, enabling them to advance rapidly when roads were available.

I also ordered most units in northern Luzon to try to make their way south as I was already envisioning War Plan Orange 3 or the retreat and entrenchment into the Bataan Peninsula. Per our pre-war planning and wargames, I deemed it the only solution in the face of overwhelming Japanese local air and naval superiority. I did not entertain much hope for the future, as the last few messages from the high command stateside told of landings on Oahu and the loss of Pearl Harbor. Guam had also been occupied (or in the process of) by that time, and most

American-mandated islands in the Pacific (Wake, Midway, Johnson Island) were either conquered or about to be… For all instances and purposes, we were completely isolated.

And to add insult to injury, I learned after the war that the Japanese knew where to strike and what we had to fight them. Our force's location, strengths, and routes were accurately plotted on their war maps. They prepared their invasion well in advance (for over a year, in fact) and had spies on the ground. Furthermore, their maps were top-notch, and their air recon efforts were as would as I would have executed them if I had been in control of the air like they were.

The rapid execution of WPO3 (War Plan Orange 3), or in more simple terms, the retreat into the Bataan Peninsula, was forced upon me by the rapid events unfolding right before our eyes. Our forces were being overwhelmed by superior numbers, ships roaming about everywhere, landings at many spots along the coastline, and commanding air force. In short, there was nothing that I could do that could change the situation and the rapid collapse that we were faced with if we stayed in Luzon and Clark Field. Bataan was in a strong defensive position (3 lines deep of fortified defenses backed up by the Corregidor Fortress) and with the supplies to last for months. In lack of better options, I ordered the troops to execute the retreat.

The imminent threat of encirclement by vastly superior numbers and complete Japanese air and naval dominance forced me to act instantly. The issue at hand was to move the army toward the west in a succession of quick maneuvers. All the while, other troops had to successfully fight a fighting-holding battle (or a fighting retreat, if you prefer).

The crux of the problem was the transition of such a big force through a bridge mountain pass called the Calumpit Bridge, just south of San Fernando, where the highway from northern Luzon to Manila joined the highway leading into Bataan. Let me tell you that General Wainright, the man on the ground, 2as able to deliver a tactical miracle. There were too many men, not enough mobile means, and not enough space to move them rapidly enough.

We found a solution to the lack of mobility by requisitioning everything that rolled and that could be used. We thus commandeered trucks, motorcycles, and all kinds of weird means as long as they went faster than walking. In a relentless ballet of back and forth (day and night), endless columns of rolling vehicles moved ammo, supplies, food, and everything in between from the capital (Manilla) to Bataan. Day and night, General Parker's command (11th and 21st Divisions, the 26th Cavalry) acted as a guard, fending off the pressing enemy. It was an operation that lacked any honor or glory, but the men did it nonetheless and with ruthless efficiency. To this day, I am proud of what my men achieved in these dire days of 1942.

Bataan was quickly organized for a protracted defense by constructing depot areas in the forests west of Lanao, developing docks at Cabcaben, Limay, and Lanao, and constructing two general hospitals. I also ordered the improvement of the road network, especially along the west coast.

As the retreat movement was achieved, I harbored no illusion about the finality of our struggle. We were isolated, overwhelmed, and outnumbered, with no real prospect of a rescue for months to come.

The naval battle of the Marianas, March 16th, 1942

The two American ships plowed the lazy waves of the Pacific, steaming south at full speed. Their mission had so far been a success. They were able to strike back at the damned Japanese. Both vessels had been ordered to steam toward the Mariana Islands of Tinian and Saipan and to bombard the airfield and harbor installations.

Old battleship Oregon and modern cruiser New Orleans had been in transit toward Guam when the war was declared. They were steaming east of the island chain on their final approach toward the American base when they were notified of the Japanese invasion on the 9th of March. The battle had been swift, and the small garrison was easily overwhelmed by the Japs. So, Oregon's captain received some final orders from the admiral in charge in Guam to attack the Japanese islands in the northern Marianas and then to steam full speed toward Australia to rendezvous with other remnants of the beleaguered Allied fleets.

Oregon was not a modern ship by any of the standards of the day. By the end of the First World War, it remained in service, and the ship was modernized in the 1920s and then again in the 1930s to improve its stability and also for conversion from steam-power to diesel-powered engines. Even with its improvements, the ship was still outdated; thus, it was more or less considered a coastal defense dreadnought rather than a high-seas battleship. With the rising tensions with Japan, it was sent to the Far East as a vessel to be used in the shallow waters of the Philippines. It was first supposed to stop at Guam and then head for Manilla Harbor. It would, of course, never get there as the war stole a march on it.

The ship in Oregon's wake was the heavy cruiser New Orleans. The New Orleans class was the last series of U.S. cruisers completed to the limitations of the Washington Naval Treaty of 1922 and designed not to exceed the 10,000-ton standard.

It sported three triple turrets of 203 mm guns and was well-armored for a vessel of his type. It wouldn't stand long against a Nipponese battleship, but it was designed to duel with smaller ships of the Imperial Navy.

The two U.S. Navy ships thus re-routed their trajectory and headed full speed toward Saipan and Tinian, which they reached on the 13th

and 14th. Luckily for them, the Japanese had not planned or expected any American ships in the area, so they didn't have many planes that could attack or recon. And so, by the time Oregon belched its shells at Tinian Island's harbor, the surprise was complete for the Japanese. The damage inflicted by both US vessels was significant on Tinian and Saipan half a day later. Both harbors were put out of commission for several weeks, and most of the planes were destroyed on the ground. Hailed as one of the first Allied victories of the war, the story would have been perfect for American morale if it had ended there and the two ships had been able to sail away into the horizon.

But the Imperial Navy was not about to let the enemy roam into its realm unchecked for long. Just as the first shells landed in Tinian, some panicked Japanese radio calls were received in Peleliu, the main harbor on Palau island, where a powerful task force was anchored, awaiting the follow-up operation in Mindanao (for the invasion of the Celebes and New Guinea).

The five ships force rapidly steamed northwest to intercept the U.S. Navy ships. Some planes were also dispatched to the northern Marianas either to attack the enemy or find the American's whereabouts.

The force was headed by Admiral Kondo and was led by a mighty battleship called the Tosa. The vessel was supposed to be destroyed under the terms of the Washington Naval Conference disarmament treaty of 1922. Still, Japan was able to fake its destruction and mascaraed an older pre-dreadnought battleship in its place and sunk it in front of Tokyo bay. Thus, the Imperial Navy fooled the international observers who had traveled to Japan to verify the ship's destruction as per the treaty's obligations.

The great boat was even modernized in great secrecy in 1935. It was not Japan's most powerful ship, but it was close. Its displacement was 41 000 tons, and it was armed with three triple turrets 404mm

naval guns. It used to have a sister ship called the Kaga (one of the flattops in the Pearl Harbor attack), but it was converted to a carrier in the 1920s. The rest of the Jap task force was not too shabby either. Two heavy cruisers (the Nachi and the Furataka), the light cruiser Nagara, and a destroyer.

Kondo's orders were to intercept and sink the Americans. With intense air search operations and several submarines also put in to find the U.S. vessels, the Imperial Navy was finally rewarded with a sighting late on the 15th of March. The Japanese admiral did not waste any time and ordered his ships to engage the enemy. The Imperial Navy task force was able to connect with the two American raiders by dusk on the 16th of March. A short but intense naval battle followed. It was the first surface action of the war apart from the Pearl Harbor duel between the Combined Fleet's battleships (Yamato and his brothers) against the Diamond Head fortifications.

The action started from a long distance, as only the battlewagons were able to fire from so far away (over 30 kilometers). Tosa's guns packed a lot more punch (and range) than Oregon's, so it could fire from a greater distance without the U.S. ship being able to counter. But the Nipponese ship did not score any long-range hits, by which time Oregon was able to fire its guns at the Furataka that moved faster toward the Americans.

A hit landed on the Japanese cruiser, destroying one of its 200mm gun turrets and starting a major fire that would see its sailor try to fight it off for most of the day's battle.

The Nachi and Nagara kept the American ships busy exchanging broadsides. At the same time, the destroyer was able to advance into torpedo range after twenty minutes of the engagement and fired its weapons at the New Orleans. The U.S. vessel was seriously hit amidship by two of them. A tremendous explosion rocked the cruiser. It lost its engine, so it was dead in the water. It continued pouring shells into the Furataka and Nachi (both Japanese cruisers got moderately damaged to that point), but everyone knew it was doomed. A ship without an engine was prey because it couldn't dodge.

After an hour or so of fire exchange, the mighty Tosa finally got into short-range and positioned itself to loosen an earth-shattering broadside at Oregon. While the Nipponese ship approached, the American vessel lodged two severe hits on the Japanese battleship while the imperial sailors continued to miss.

But at short range, the Japs could only miss for so long, and the nine 407mm guns finally fired simultaneously and found the range on their enemy. The guns belched their powerful shells, followed by a tremendous shockwave that churned the water right by the vessel and created a large, conic-rippled wake in front of the Tosa.

The red tracer shells arced rapidly, and eight out of nine slammed into the American ship. Darkness was almost complete by then, and the shell's impact produced a blinding light, only increased by the corresponding explosion in Oregon. The U.S. ship was old, and while it had been modernized, it was still an outdated armor design, so it did not react really well to the impact of the giant armor-piercing shells.

The Japanese ordinance sliced through Oregon's deck, sides, and bottom. The funnel, the weapon magazine, and the fuel reserve were hit almost simultaneously. The impacts created a catastrophic chain explosion that the aged vessel could simply not endure. When the bright flash created by the hit faded, nothing was left on the waves but floating debris and scattered patches of burning oil.

After another ten minutes, New Orleans was also finished. The Japanese ships shelled it to oblivion in an orgy of violent, raging pandemonium.

The Japanese advance to Singapore, March 11th to March 28th, 1942

Ten days into the start of the war, the writing already seemed on the wall as to the result of the Malaya Campaign. The defeat of Allied troops at the Battle of Jitra by Japanese forces, supported by tanks moving south from Thailand on March 8th and the rapid advance of the Japanese inland from their Kota Bharu beachhead on the northeast coast, overwhelmed the northern defenses.

After the destruction of the only naval force that could bar the Imperial Navy from supporting the Japanese soldiers (Force Z), the Allies were left without any real maritime presence in the theater. Thus, the British could not challenge the Imperial Navy in the area. With nothing of substance left in terms of air strength following the heavy air battles and airstrikes of the first few days of the struggle, the Japanese could and did bomb the Allied ground troops mercilessly.

The Indian 3rd Corps and a few British units offered stiff resistance to the Japanese. But they got overwhelmed on the flanks and by relentless bombings. The battle ended up being a dead end for the Allies, who had to relinquish the coastline in Khota Baru and south of it. In short, the IJA held all the cards.

While General Yamashita's forces possessed a comfortable superiority in terms of soldiers, the difference makers were battle experience, airpower, and Japanese armored units since the Allied in Malaya had none to oppose them; IJA units had been fighting in the Second Sino-Japanese War for three years already when they embarked on their Malaya campaign. The Japanese moved a lot quicker than their opponents as they made good use of bicycles and light armored trucks. They were thus able to move on native paths and in places where the Allied commanders didn't think they could, or at least not as fast as they did.

By the end of the second week of March, all of Northern Malaya was under imperial control. At the same time, Thailand followed right after by surrendering all its forces and signing a treaty of alliance with Japan, completely negating any forces that could have hampered the Japanese forces' supply lines. Kuala Lumpur fell the next day the treaty between the two countries was signed. From there, the final prize of Singapore lay only two hundred miles from the lead Japanese units.

By March 20th, the Allies established a new line of defense in the state of Johore centered on the New Zealander 2nd Division, hoping to stem the enemy tide that was splashing all across the peninsula. They also were supported by a dozen hodgepodge Allied units, including several remnants of Indian divisions, defeated and broken in earlier battles.

There the Japanese were inflicted their first major defeat in Malaya thanks to the Kiwi's stubborn resistance (in a town called Gemas) and excellent fighting spirit. The battle happened near a critical Bridge that got destroyed in the fighting and where the IJA suffered heavy casualties trying to cross the river on makeshift boats and barges. The situation was only improved when the imperial combat engineers were finally able to put a pontoon bridge together half a day later.

All the while, further Japanese landings took place at Endau, outflanking the Allied position. On March 27th, the fighting troops received permission from the commander of the American-British-Dutch-Australian Command, General Arthur Percival, to retreat to the Island of Singapore, where they hoped to execute a successful siege defense of the Malay capital.

After exploding a giant mine on March 28th to destroy the causeway linking Singapore to the mainland, the last British, New Zealander, and Indian forces left Malaya to hunker down in the fortress city.

The Battle for Malaya, Thailand, and the peninsula did not even last a month and ended in an unequivocal defeat for the Allies. Over forty-five thousand fighting soldiers were killed, captured, and left behind as the desperate retreat to Singapore was executed.

On April 1st, Japanese forces started to probe the Singapore defenses and hoped for a swift victory. By then, the Imperial Air Force bombarded the city daily. The outlook did not look good for Percival's men and their future.

Battleship Yamato, Pearl Harbor April 1st, 1942

As the magnificent Yamato battleship slowly entered Pearl Harbor, Grand Admiral Isoroku Yamamoto could not help but feel proud and satisfied. The Empire had done it! It had taken the Hawaiian Islands.

What was now reality had been far from a foregone conclusion when the Combined Fleet started its trek across the Pacific under total secrecy and radio silence. He remembered the dread and nervousness he'd felt at the time. The Imperial Navy was powerful, but Japan could not build ships rapidly and didn't have unlimited resources like the Americans. As a consequence, it could not afford losses or failed operations.

There were even standing orders in the Navy about husbanding ammunition and being smart with how they needed to be expended. Losing a fleet carrier would also be tantamount to a small disaster for the Empire. A few were under construction or in the planning stages, but Japan would be lucky to produce a full fleet carrier every two years. Some smaller escort carriers were also in the process of being made, but Yamamoto suspected that it wouldn't be enough compared to the American shipbuilding capability.

So, the almost bloodless victory that the Combined Fleet obtained in Hawaii was satisfying to the Grand Admiral. They'd lost only a few planes (three dozen) and were able to recuperate or save most of their experienced pilots. Some of the warships had been "bruised" by the duel with the Diamond Head defenses, but nothing that warranted a return to Japan for major repairs. The ship that got the worst of the exchange on the Jap side was the Nagato dreadnought, and it was being repaired within Pearl Harbor itself. Looking in the ship's direction, Isoroku could even see the welding flashes of the repair crews at work as his ship slid into port.

The rest of the island chain conquest had gone pretty smoothly. After numerous air raids, the silencing of Diamond Head, and several landings across Oahu, the Japanese Army was able to secure the area. Intense battles occurred around Kaneohe base and at Kahuku point, where several American Units had entrenched themselves. Honolulu had fallen like a ripe fruit once the Diamond Head fortress surrendered on the 6th of March.

Kauai was stormed almost without any casualties, as the place was garrisoned only by an under-strength American battalion. Maui was much the same, although an intense battleship shore bombardment had been needed to reduce some American resistance around Wailea. Molokai was taken without a fight, as well.

The most intense battle had been on the big island, where a complete U.S. division was entrenched. They had several planes and had been well-equipped with guns (artillery), so the struggle proved a little more difficult than the rest.

But the result had been a foregone conclusion the minute the U.S. Navy retired from the area. Yamamoto couldn't fault them for doing so, for the Americans hadn't entertained any aircraft carriers in the Pacific at the moment of the Japanese attack. So it would have been pure folly to charge to the attack with a surface fleet against all the ships and planes of the Combined Fleet.

After all, Japan had more ships than the USA at that moment, more aircraft carriers, and more battleships. And now, the Japanese Army was sending more troops as planned. Additional plane shipments were scheduled to arrive soon. The Grand Admiral hoped that within a couple more months, the Hawaii position would be a very difficult nut to crack.

It would need to be because if his understanding of the future American strategy was correct, they would come right for Pearl Harbor and try to wrest it from the Empire. Only then could they contemplate a Pacific campaign.

The rest of the war was going quite well, according to the reports he'd received; in fact, it was going exceedingly well... Miles beyond his wildest dreams. He knew the Allies were not adequately prepared for war compared to Japan. Still, he hadn't appreciated the weakness of their resolve, the inadequacy of their equipment or supply reserves, the lousy positioning of their units, or the unexplainable sluggishness of their command structure.

The results were there to see in all their glory: The Japanese troops were in front of Singapore and laid siege to the fortress after conquering Thailand and Malaysia. Most of the Philippines were in Japanese hands, except for the Bataan Peninsula and the Corregidor fortress, where General Macarthur had entrenched himself with over 80,000 men. While the famous American leader would continue to resist for a long while, Yamamoto knew that he would eventually have to surrender, for no hope of rescue was even close to happening. In the depths of Asia, he was stranded thousands of miles from America and Australia, with scores of aggressive Japanese warships in between to prevent any relief effort.

And the final, most important prize was within Japan's grasp. The Dutch East Indies were almost defenseless. Imperial forces were now moving toward it to take the essential areas like Sarawak in Borneo (oil), Java, Sumatra (oil, rubber), Ambon, Timor, and the Celebes.

And the last part of Yamamoto's grand plan was finally also unfolding: The conquest of most Pacific Islands. Wake, Midway, and Johnson islands had already fallen in simple operations by small fleets since they'd been mostly under-garrisoned except for Wake, which had a half battalion. Some casualties were reported there, but nothing major, and besides, the warships had ended all resistance since they'd been able to have all of the island's landmass under their guns. The Allied forces soon surrendered.

The rest of the Pacific's objectives were numerous but attainable. The Gilbert Islands (already being invaded), American Samoa, New Britain, the Solomon Islands, and New Caledonia.

He'd dispatched the fleet carriers Soryu, and Hiryu, about 15 destroyers, and four heavy cruisers to support the operations. A few days ago, the ships had steamed out of Pearl and were scheduled first to help with the Gilbert Island's operation but were due south to the Coral Sea, where he expected some Australian resistance to Japanese moves.

It was a bit of a risk not to keep the powerful ships in Pearl, for the Americans were sure to come to Hawaii, but he estimated that he had some time before the U.S. Navy transferred all of its ships to the Pacific. And besides, he still kept the Akagi, Kaga, Shokaku, and Zuikaku carriers in Hawaii, plus some mighty surface guns with Yamato and other ships.

The Japanese occupation of the Gilbert Islands
March 11-26th, 1942

On February 2nd, 1942, Operation Gi (for the Gilbert Islands) was ordered by Grand Admiral Yamamoto. The Japanese 4th Fleet thus departed from Truk, the Imperial headquarters of the South Seas Mandate.

The flagship was the minelayer Tagigata. The operation included the minelayers Tsugaru Tenyo Maru, in addition to light cruisers Tokiwa, Nagata, Asanagi, and the Yūnagi. The Chitose seaplane tender was also sent to provide air cover. On March 7th, 1942, Admiral Okinoshima (task force commander) received the signal from Hawaii to set forth for the operation. Okinoshima arrived at Jaluit in the Marshalls and embarked on an SNLF elite naval battalion from the 51st Guards Force and two more regular army battalions transported to the islands a month prior. The 4th fleet departed from Jaluit on March 8th.

The Gilbert Islands were operated under a British mandate and were administered loosely under the guise of a colonial administration. The United Kingdom, which had other fish to fry in the world, did not even stop one second to think about garrisoning the islands, even if they had an enormous strategic value in terms of positioning in the Central Pacific. It was just beyond British capability in 1942.

So, for the three Japanese battalions, it became a simple occupation without any bloodshed. The vital islands/atolls of Makin, Tarawa, Abaiang, Marakei, and Abedama were thus filled with Nipponese soldiers. The Grand Admiral wanted the Islands for defense, and the troops were immediately put to work. Some engineers were also supposed to eventually be shipped to the area to build a few airstrips. Within the next few years, bunkers, defenses, airfields, and even small, purpose-built harbors would spring up in the Gilbert, and America would eventually have to toil hard to liberate them.

In the meantime, a seaplane base was rapidly organized on Makin Atoll Lagoon to have good air coverage and reconnaissance in the area.

The whole affair took a little over two weeks but was nothing more than a footnote in the grand scheme of things. The war would eventually come to the area, but not in 1942.

CHAPTER 3

7th Air Fleet, April 1st, 1942

Commander Genda was walking between the busy workers rebuilding the large hangars for the airfield in Oahu called Hickam Field. There was no mistaking it; the Japanese airstrike had done significant damage.

After weeks of work on the former American base, the airfield was becoming operational. The tarmac had been repaired quickly, but everything else had needed more time. Gasoline facilities had to be rebuilt since they'd been bombed and so had exploded, most of the hangars had been burnt down to the ground, and the airbase equipment had been destroyed.

The Army had even asked for the Navy's help to clear the numerous wreckages strewn about and find more machinery. They requisitioned everything that could be found on the island, as the shipment of construction machinery had been delayed. The convoy ship had left Japan a week or so ago but had not arrived in Pearl yet.

He crossed an extensive line of flying welding sparks, walked some more between a bunch of large crates containing materials for the construction effort, and finally got to his destination. The construction maelstrom opened into one of the repaired runways, where a newly built hangar was also standing. It housed the men of the 7th Air Fleet or at least the nucleus of what would be the 7th Air Fleet. The new unit was to be the main force to defend the island when the Americans came back to attack it.

The hangar was new, so it looked pristine. Several Zero fighters were parked just outside of it, and many mechanics worked around them doing some maintenance. Other aircraft, mainly Val dive-bombers, could also be seen on the other side of the hangar, with more men working on them.

A bit further out, a bunch of pilots ran in a group, singing some military song. The pilots were busy training and staying in shape. The 7th was a joint effort by the Army and Navy to organize Oahu's air defense force. The plan was to make a unit, integrate Army pilots into the Imperial Navy's defenses, and train them for sea operations.

Admiral Yamamoto (and Genda, of course) would certainly have liked only to have Navy pilots for the defenses of the Hawaiian Islands. Alas, it was not possible because they didn't have enough of them. The Army had the bulk of the aircraft and the pilots, and the Navy had only the ones supposed to operate from aircraft carriers.

With the estimated size of the eventual U.S. Navy attacks, the Grand Admiral had rapidly concluded, in his planning even before the invasion itself, that Japan would need many more planes than just the ones the Navy could supply from its aircraft carriers, as good as they may be.

The USA had a good number of carriers and was sure to make more, so when they finally moved to retake Oahu, the Empire would need land-based planes to keep air and naval supremacy on the islands.

As per Genda and Isoroku's discussion (since they conquered Oahu) they even figured that if they could put enough Army planes/pilots (and trained them) on Hickam field and the other airfields being built across the island chain, they would keep the Yanks away for a long while.

Their calculations were relatively straightforward. The best and largest aircraft carriers could embark sixty to seventy planes. And even if the

Americans built big enough to have 100-planes carriers, it would still be a small portion of what Japan could bring on the Hawaii Island airfields. The plan was to have over 800 naval-capable planes by the time the U.S. showed itself for battle. So, as per Yamamoto's own words, "having 800 planes was like having ten or twelve additional carriers with which to battle the U.S. Navy".

Genda wholeheartedly agreed with the idea, except that getting the Army to collaborate fully with the Navy and be adequately trained would not be easy. Making a good carrier pilot took at least twenty-four months of hard training, so it was not a given that Japan would have the time to prepare all the flyers for when the enemy came at them. At least, he thought, they didn't have to train them in carrier landing operations, as the whole point of the 7th Air Fleet was to have naval-capable planes based on land.

He figured he would have suitable pilots within six months and outstanding ones within a year. In between, they would be able to be part of the fighting, but unfortunately, if the U.S. attacked before they were ready, they would just have to learn on the go while fighting in the air and sea.

USS Wahoo (U-239)

Marshall Islands, April 3rd, 1942

Lieutenant Commander Jim Cloutier lowered the periscope and ordered his men to prepare to fire. "First officer. Fire." The skipper said in a calm voice.

And with that simple order, the USS Wahoo sent its first torpedo in anger at the Japanese. The ship was in the Marshall Atoll chain of islands near Kwajalein. The Imperial Navy entertained a large base in that area, and it was a given that some of the ships that attacked Pearl Harbor came from there.

USS Wahoo was a Gato-Class submarine, the first real fleet sub for the U.S. Navy. It was a 75-day cruise ship that could operate independently across the Pacific theater. It was small in terms of displacement (1500 tons) but packed 24 torpedoes and a 76mm deck gun.

The Wahoo and several of its brothers were at sea when the Japanese attacked and invaded Pearl Harbor. After the events, it was ordered to attack Japanese shipping in any way. Unfortunately for commander Cloutier, his sub had been out of position relative to the Pearl Harbor battle since it was cruising in the Gilbert Islands.

After he figured out that the war had started, he quickly ordered the sub toward the Marshall Islands and its Kwajalein base. He aimed to score hits on the damned enemy and see what they were up to.

They'd made good speed toward the Atoll and finally arrived two days ago. They'd taken the time to recon the area and determine what the enemy had.

The base was an important hub for the Japanese Navy. It hosted a port facility and several small airfields on Kwajalein and the neighboring islands. Cloutier and his men had also spotted several destroyers operating patrols. They presumed that they were checking for submarines, but they'd stayed far enough away to remain undetected.

And today, a nice plum target had shown itself in the Wahoo's periscope: a large troop transport escorted by what seemed to be a light cruiser and a couple of destroyers. The lieutenant commander did not know where they came from or their destination, but he figured it was time to hit the Japs.

As the torpedo's wake progressed toward the enemy ship (he'd brought the periscope back up to check on the weapon's trajectory), he counted the seconds to its destination. 5... 4... 3... 2... 1...

A powerful explosion rocked the Japanese transport ship, blossoming into a large pillar of flame and smoke-laden debris that skyrocketed in the air. "Dive now!" he yelled. Time was of the essence, for if one thing was certain after they hit the enemy boat, planes and ships would look for them and try to sink the Wahoo.

The standard defense against the destroyers that would try to locate them, and fire depth charges was to dive and try to get out of the area as fast as possible.

Sometimes, when the enemy ships picked them up on their sonar (that was how Cloutier figured it would be since it was his first real war and he had only trained on the tactics), the trick was to stop moving and shut down the engines to lie in wait.

After some minutes, the enemy ships rapidly overtook the area where the Wahoo had been. Another aspect of submarine warfare was that destroyers were relatively faster than the subs in terms of speed. For example, the Wahoo's top speed was 21 knots, while the average Japanese destroyer was thirty-seven to 40 knots.

Whatever the Americans did, they would be overtaken by their enemy, so better play dead or slip away slowly and as deeply as possible.

Anti-submarine technology was still in its infancy in the early years of World War Two. So Cloutier was not overly worried, as he'd seen the report on Japanese sonar technology. It was miles behind the most modern Western types.

The all-quiet order had already been given across the ship, for any noise could be picked up by the sailors' listening devices on the destroyers. No one moved as they slowly started to hear the enemy engine approaching and then passing overhead. It also didn't take long for them to hear the characteristic sound of the sonar ping that rang like a small bell on the sub's surface and surrounding sea bottom. The sonar's concept was that the ship trying to locate a submarine sent a sound wave and could detect a ship from how it reflected the prey it was looking for.

Cloutier's best defense was to drop as deep as possible (in this case they had dived to the bottom, which wasn't too deep) and stop moving, so his vessel would blend in its surroundings for the sonar operator.

Suddenly, a loud but muffled explosion was heard, and the sub shook perceptibly. The Nipponese sailors were trying to get a lucky hit, as they hadn't put a lock on the Wahoo yet.

But luckily for the U.S. men, the subs dropped charges too far away from them. The Japanese destroyers tried to locate the Wahoo for another two hours but couldn't get a lock. They dropped more depth charges, hoping for a lucky hit, but the Imperial Navy's standing orders on husbanding ammunition and resources won in the end. When darkness fell on the same day, Captain Cloutier ordered the ship up to the surface, and they left the area for the high sea.

The sub had a rendezvous to get to; the Navy High Command had ordered all submarines to Australia. They would first try to stop at American Samoa to refuel and then head for the northern Australian coast.

Davao, Philippines (Mindanao Island), March 17th, 1942

Takashi Onishi whistled softly, working diligently on his plane's 20mm cannon. He was cleaning it in preparation for the battle planned the very next day. They were to escort a paratrooper operation to the northern Celebes, specifically to the Minahasa Peninsula, over the town of Menado. He was happy because he had just received a letter from Kikiko, the girl he had corresponded with since his China days. They were engaged, and he longed to be with her and return to Japan. She was a lovely girl in Sasebo. Her family was a prominent one who approved of their potential union. Onishi would not have been able to court the girl if he hadn't been a successful pilot in the Chinese air war. He thanked the high heavens every day for his luck. He was from a poor traditional samurai family from Tosa province and could not have hoped to date a girl of that caliber if it hadn't been for his military service. He'd been lucky to be posted to the city for a few months back in 1939 and, as such, had met the girl's father and family. They'd approved of their potential union. As a military officer with some fame attached to his name, he'd been given a chance and had not wasted it. The girl corresponded with him almost daily, and he did the same whenever possible, but army life was difficult, especially on a campaign. But he'd been fortunate on this day; the mail (an infrequent occurrence since the beginning of March) had finally arrived.

The girl talked about daily life (she was still in school) and how the war's privations were difficult. He kept thinking about the answer he would write her later in the evening.

The war was going well for Japan, and Takashi was at its forefront with his seven victories. His last two had been over the Philippines, one against a P-40 Warhawk and the second against an aging and outdated Brewster Buffalo from the Dutch Air Force.

The battle was not over on Luzon Island, where he'd started his war; the Allied forces resisted bitterly in the Bataan Peninsula, and there seemed to be no end in sight. But the need for fighter cover had greatly diminished now that the enemy aircraft were thousands of miles from there. The Japanese imperial forces had taken most of the main bases and airfields that could have been used to help Macarthur's troops. And besides, the Allies had their hands full everywhere else, like in Borneo, Malaya, or the rest of the Dutch East Indies.

Since the start of the war over three weeks ago, the enemy had not even attempted an attack on their base, either in Formosa or Davao, where Onishi's squadron had been ordered to. The airfield they occupied was still in the process of being repaired and upgraded. American forces had owned it before the successful invasion of Davao at the beginning of the month.

As a consequence, a sort of complacency had established itself. Victory had given too much confidence to the Japanese. Contrary to the U.S. or even the British, the Empire was only starting to equip its force with radar. Only the top ship had it (Yamato) in March and April 1942. There was consequently no warning that several B-17 bombers were approaching at a high altitude since there was no plane above to watch for approaching enemies. The Japanese commander had deemed it unnecessary.

The American bombers were spotted at the last moment on their final approach when a sharp Nipponese lookout noticed the ten black dots in the sky.

The U.S. Army's 11th Bomber squadron, flying from Java in the Dutch East Indies, had been ordered on a raiding mission to Davao. Allied intelligence knew of Japanese preparations for a move against the Celebes and other locations southward.

And so, they'd flown as high as possible and under complete radio silence until such time that they got to their target. The American pilots then dropped to an altitude to aim and launch their bombloads efficiently, thus finally helping the Japanese spot them.

Takashi heard the alarm sirens at the same time as everyone else and only had the time to look up before the whistling sounds of bombs dropping to the ground were heard. He was standing up on the side wing, painting an American flag on the fuselage to indicate that he'd just scored another air victory. The next few seconds became a blur for the Japanese pilot as large explosions rocked the airfield. The ground shook so hard that he fell from his plane on the airfield tarmac. One of the large hangars near him, which had luckily survived the imperial invasion weeks earlier, was hit by a couple of powerful bombs and exploded outward, flattening everything within a fifteen-meter radius. That included Onishi and his fighter, both thrown into the air like rag dolls.

The fighter broke into two pieces and shattered itself on another hangar just a few meters away, igniting it with its flaming and exploding gasoline tank. Takashi was favored by lady luck that day and was thrown several meters into the air into a small water pond nearby. The airfield was built on an old farm, and the pilot fell into one of the old animal watering holes.

It helped him survive the crash since he hit the water, so he avoided hurting himself on the hard ground and was submerged long enough for the rolling flames of both hangar's explosions to pass over him.

By the time Onishi regained his bewildered senses and pushed himself back up to the surface to gasp for some air, the fierce pandemonium was expanding to other areas of the airfield. Still stunned, he tried to focus upward, where the enemy bombers were cruising. They seemed to circle around the airport, and he estimated they were at about 20,000 feet.

A sense of deep rage and shame invaded Takashi at the same time. How dare the Americans attack them! And how shameful for him and his pilot comrades to have been caught unaware! He looked around to find a fighter since he was destroyed, still fiercely burning in the raging inferno of the former hangar. He spotted a lone Zero aircraft lodged neatly in between two large fires. It seemed untouched by the fire.

Getting out of the water, dripping all over, he ran as fast as he could toward the plane. He was sure the B-17s were circling in a wide turn to come back over Davao to attack again. He could see them high in the sky and imagined their arrogant smiles on their approach at the defenseless base; no Japanese aircraft seemed up in the air. Onishi resolved to take care of that problem.

He got to the Zero, jumped on its wing, opened the canopy, and slid into the cockpit. He immediately started the aircraft and, without waiting for the engine's normal warming-up sequence as he'd learned in training, began rolling right away, pushing the throttle to its maximum. It was against all regulations and could literally kill the plane's engine, but Takashi didn't care. The Zero was doomed anyway if it didn't lift off the ground. The imperial engineers and maintenance people could bitch about it after the battle if he survived.

The fighter protested loudly as it groaned to full power, and Onishi finally wrested it from the ground and into the air. Never before had he taken a plane so fast in the sky. Once there, he continued to push his machine to the maximum and could finally feel the engine's groaning subside as he picked up altitude.

By the time he was at twenty thousand feet he'd estimated the B-17s to be a few moments before, he didn't have to wait long to see if he'd guessed right. Tracers soon shot out of the flying fortresses as they peppered the area around his Zero with tracers. Luckily, none of the enemy's shells and bullets hit him, so he was able to make his attack run at the big bomber that approached his targeting sight. About fifty meters from it (a very short-range distance), he loosened a long burst of his 20mm cannons. The red tracers arced and curved in the sky and connected with the bomber's port wing, which split in two. It had the immediate effect of sending the American aircraft into a tumble. It spiraled to its doom for a few seconds and then blossomed on the ground into a mushroom of fire and black smoke. Onishi didn't know it yet because he didn't have enough experience with the big lumbering bombers, but it was a one-in-a-million shot. Killing a B-17 in one pass was something to behold and greatly dependent on luck.

He then turned his plane into a semi-loop to dodge incoming enemy fire. The American ordinance zipped harmlessly just over his right wing. He leveled his fighter again to fire at another American bomber that was busy unloading the next set of bombs at Davao's airfield. He could even see the bombs spurt from the plane's opened bays.

Takashi sent another fiery tracer burst that again arced toward the American plane. It hit the side fuselage and created significant damage, but the B-17 would have survived if not for one of Onishi's shells hitting one of the bombs streaming out toward Davao. Another lucky shot. The consequent explosion rocked the plane and smashed it from its underbelly, opening it like a tin can. Takashi saw the thing scatter in pieces as he thundered above the stricken aircraft. He even watched as a couple of men (probably the side gunners) were expelled from the debris mass, on fire and gesticulating frantically to their death below.

By the time he was done and turning again, the rest of the American aircraft were finished unloading their bombs and veered southward to make good their escape. Onishi wanted nothing more than to pursue them and continue to kill the dastardly enemies, but his Zero engine was spurting flames and the smoke it was creating obscured his view. The machine was also losing power, and he decided he'd done enough for the day. He'd pushed the fighter too hard and too fast, and the bill was now due.

He dropped his plane toward the ground to find a place to land. With the destroyed airport below, it would prove to be a challenge in itself.

The invasion of the Celebes, March 18-23rd, 1942

The men of the 1st SNLF battalion threw themselves at the sky toward the Dutch airfield of Menado. The Japanese transport planes flew high above the northern Celebes, also called the Minahasa Peninsula. The battalion's mission: secure the major airfield in the area. The white parachutes filled the blue horizon over the Allied installations, and it didn't take long for the Dutch soldiers to fight back. Some AA guns (anti-aircraft) were present at the airfield, so they shot the planes, disgorging their angry tracers at the Japanese soldiers, but they didn't hit anything. The troops themselves (there were about 800 men in the Menado area) fired with all they had as well, and they killed several Jap paratroopers. But the 1st SNLF was a thousand-strong unit, so they rapidly overwhelmed their enemy's position. Within an hour of the drop, fighting broke out everywhere in the Menado area, town, and airfield. Two hours after the drop, Japanese planes arrived, struck Dutch positions, and strafed the airfield. Then, some heavy surface units (battleship Haruna plus heavy cruisers Nachi and Furataka) joined in and finished the job. By four in the afternoon, all Allied forces in the Menado area had been killed, injured, or surrendered.

The Rikusentai units were elite Nipponese Marine units grouped in battalion-level formations named after the three naval districts in Japan. Some of them were paratroopers in unit's setup in late 1941 as war loomed and their usefulness appeared likely. They were lightly armed but very well trained, and thus, the Menado operation was perfect for them. The Imperial Navy was about to land a regiment of soldiers, but the battle was already over by the time the Army men arrived. While the Marine paratroopers had received heavy losses, it was still considered a success by the high command.

The Minahasa Peninsula (the northern part of the Celebes) was an essential area for the Japanese to control for their continued push into the Dutch East Indies, as it offered a modern harbor with good natural bays to serve as bases for seaplanes and flying boats.

Dutch forces had also constructed two airfields nearby. One was in Langoan and another in Manado, which was still under construction when the war broke out.

Battleship Haruna was accompanied by aircraft carrier Ryujo and five destroyers (Amatsukaze, Jintsu, Hyashio, Natsushio, Kurushio, and Oyashio). Another powerful fleet was doubling back to the area to reinforce the invaders should they be needed. It was headed by battleship Tosa, the victor of the naval battle of the Marianas, where the American battlewagon Oregon and the New Orleans heavy cruiser had been sunk two days prior.

With the conquest of Menado and the northern Peninsula done and over on the 18th and 19th, the Japanese forces prepared their follow-up moves to central and Southern Celebes.

By the 20th, things were organized enough in Menado that the Imperial Navy, now fully reinforced with the Tosa task force, launched itself southward at Kendari. The airfield that the SNLF forces had just conquered was also finalized. The Jap air force put it to good use, launching strikes at the city and other targets, like the vital island of Ambon and the island of Timor.

During the night between the 20th and the 21st, the Imperial Navy continued its nighttime amphibious landing tactic. They used darkness to cover their moves. At dawn, a powerful airstrike struck Kendari while the 451st Regiment landed the night before consolidated its gains. By ten in the morning, air recon reported Kendari on fire and lightly defended. It was thus deemed safe to give the go-ahead to the Tosa task force to bombard the Dutch Army position north of the town. Casualties rapidly mounted on the Allied side, military and civilians alike.

The 22nd of March saw some truly heavy combat between the beleaguered Royal forces and the Imperial Army. By dusk that day, it became obvious that the Allies would not hold for long. They had no air cover, and the Japanese naval guns pounded them into oblivion.

Following a demand to surrender from Japanese General Takahashi the very next morning at dawn, the Dutch forces laid down their arms.

Admiral Nagumo bombs American soil April 7th, 1942

Admiral Chuichi Nagumo, commander of the Kiddo Butai (Japan's main carrier group), was feeling nervous and confident at the same time. It was a weird feeling, and he couldn't help but shake the fear of losing his ships, even if Japan's Imperial Navy had so far brushed all resistance before it.

The task force he commanded was powerful, yet he wished he'd stayed safe in Hawaii. He was not worried about his personal safety but felt that the country could not afford to lose any of its large fleet flattops; he was currently heading into the teeth of the enemy. The raid that Grand Admiral Yamamoto had ordered him to execute was bold to the extreme. Nagumo considered it pure folly.

The mission was relatively straightforward in its objectives yet complex in its execution. Nagumo was to sail Kiddo Butai in strike range of San Diego and launch several attacks (as much as needed) to destroy air defenses (airfields, planes) and, most importantly, the oil and dock facilities. Japanese intelligence knew for a fact (they'd placed many spies in California before the war, and several were still reporting) that the unavoidable American buildup was or would occur there. So far, no aircraft carrier had been reported anywhere close to the city. Still, it was a given that the U.S. Navy would re-transfer some surface ships and carriers to the Pacific now that it was utterly defenseless against the Imperial Navy.

And they would come to San Diego for its logistical capabilities and the size of its protected harbor.

The Grand Admiral had given Nagumo a very powerful task force to execute his mission. It was centered around the four fleet carriers Akagi, Kaga, Shokaku, and Zuikaku. The surface escort (mostly there for anti-aircraft purposes as the plan did not entail any possibility of a surface action or getting anywhere close to the Californian coast to shell it) was also quite potent with battleships Hiei and Kirishima, four heavy cruisers (Chikuma, Maya, Myoko, and Tone), five light cruisers and ten destroyers for anti-submarine operations. The task force had 300 planes to strike San Diego in what was hoped to be a surprise attack on the harbor and its adjoining facilities.

Nagumo was standing on the bridge of his flagship, Akagi, the most prestigious and powerful of all the Japanese carriers. The ship used to be a battlecruiser but had to be converted to a carrier in the 1920s. The Washington Naval Conference forced the Empire to destroy or transform the ship into something other than a big naval gunship. In a weird twist of fate, it had given Japan some mighty carriers it would not have had without the Washington restrictions. Also, Akagi's waterline armored belt was an impressive 152 mm. After all, it had been converted from a battlecruiser in construction to an aircraft carrier.

The ship looked powerful if slightly offset since it was not the typical carrier design, but Admiral Nagumo was proud to serve on it. The strike on Pearl Harbor had originated and was led by this very ship. And now, the Akagi would also execute the first attack on the American mainland.

Looking one more time at the assembled planes on the Akagi's deck (the aircraft were already hot and ready to take off), he sighed deeply to himself and then turned toward his air fleet commander, Mitsuo Fushida. "Captain, you are good to go." "Thank you, Admiral," answered the captain with a respectful bow. The other officers only listened to the quick exchange, busy as they were with their own tasks. Running a carrier was not a simple affair.

Fushida turned around and left the bridge for his Zero fighter. The order was also relayed by radio to the flight deck officer to commence takeoff operations.

Nagumo, still worried but at the same time excited to see another strike on the enemy take to the sky, turned around again to watch the brave pilots take off. In the distance, he also saw planes from Zuikaku, Shokaku, and Kaga moving and taking off from their respective decks.

The aircraft climbed off the flattops one after the other while their brothers circled the task force to wait for all of them. After half an hour of hectic activity, over three hundred planes headed west toward the skyline and another attack that would enrage America to its core.

Assault on Singapore, April 9th, 1942

Taking a deep breath, soldier Ishiro Tanaka of the 18th Imperial Army Division wondered if he would survive this attack. It was not that he was afraid to die. It was just that he was human and wanted to live to see another day. Well, if he honestly thought about it, he wasn't so keen on dying for the Empire anyway.

But his will to live was in serious jeopardy because of the assault he and his squad mates had been ordered to make. The men of the 18th that he was with were stuck in a dirty ditch in front of the Singapore defenses. The city was on an island, and for a time, it had resisted the IJA's assault because the Allied commander had retired all his men across the body of water over what was called the Johore Strait. Normal access had been destroyed by the retreating Allies when they blew up the giant causeway that linked the city to the mainland. It took time for the Nipponese forces to get organized, move the necessary artillery, and imperial engineers to make new pontoon bridges. Then, to get the men loaded for another landing, this time directly in the island city.

As per standard imperial procedure, they'd done so in the dead of night, but this time, the Allies had been waiting for them and gave them hell as they got to the shore. The Japanese Navy continued to shell the defenses, and the air force even sent a powerful night raid. Still, it had not been enough, and Tanaka's squad and others like it had been shredded as they'd exited the wild assortment of small transport ships and barges that the Army had assembled for the occasion. Ishiro didn't know how many soldiers' dead on the Japanese side of things were, but he would have been appalled by the casualty rate that even high command kept well hidden after the victorious conclusion of the battle. Over 40% of the 18th division was dead or seriously injured from their landing operations.

Still, General Yamashita was happy, as first of all, IJA commanders didn't really care about casualty levels (they had so many men anyway), and second, the 18th was ashore and fighting, giving some measure of space for the engineers to make the pontoon bridges needed for the rest of his men.

Laying on his back, Tanaka watched the red tracer shells of the imperial artillery arcing high over them to go and land in Singapore itself. The sight made him happy, and he longed to be done with the fighting and staying alive. The Japanese forces subjected the city to a non-stop bombardment since the start of the siege. While the enemy fire was unrelenting from his perspective, it had slackened in a general sense as Allied forces lost more and more men and their ammunition levels dwindled.

The whistle was blown, and the men of the 18th stirred from their muddy holes and leveled their guns at the enemy. Immediately, the Indo-British forces started to pour fire into the Jap ranks. Ishiro ran as fast as he could, yelling out of his lungs. Bent on reaching the enemy trench, he didn't look at the ground before him and slipped on a rock. He fell on the ground and rolled into a shell hole by accident. A bullet zipped by overhead. His clumsy fall saved him, but his squad mates were not so lucky, and they all got hit in some form or the other. A couple got their head blown, disappearing in a gory mist of red liquid; some more got catapulted sky-high by an enemy anti-tank shell, and Vickers-Berthier machine guns gunned down the rest.

By the time Tanaka returned to his senses (he'd been knocked out for a few seconds), he was alone. He peered his head over the hole and was rewarded by several bursts on the ground, thanks to enemy bullets fired at him. He was stuck there for the moment and decided that prudence was the better part of valor for him that day. He just hoped that the enemy soldiers in the trench would stay where they were. As long as they only tried defense, he would survive unless they fired some mortar rounds at him, or he was unlucky enough to get a shrapnel wound or some other freak way of dying on the battlefield.

Some time passed, and he lost track of it. Such was the way it went in a firefight. Time either flashed by or slowed down to a mere trickle. In this instance, the whole ordeal seemed to take forever to Tanaka as he crouched in a ball, surrounded by mud and dirty water.

Eventually, an Imperial Navy gun or other artillery unit took the trench he faced as a target and started to pepper it with heavy detonations, rocking the ground that shook like a small earthquake. Some explosions (that was why Ishiro thought it was naval ordinance) were so big that the ground, trenches, and humans that were hit skyrocketed high in the air, churning everything in their wake, showering the poor Japanese soldier hiding in his hole with dirt and gore.

A few minutes after the heavy bombardment, Tanaka could finally hear some relief coming. Another charge was directed from behind him, lifted by a loud "Banzai!" yell. When he started to see some Japanese men jump over him and run toward the enemy position, he lifted out of his hole, removing most of the accumulated dirt that was on him. He clutched his rifle as hard as possible and followed his comrades to the fight.

The rest of the battle was a confused mass of hand-to-hand struggle, mainly a one-sided massacre. The Allied soldiers, dazed, outnumbered, and shellshocked, just died because even those who tried surrendering were killed by the unforgiving Nipponese soldiers.

Tanaka, face covered in crusted and fresh blood, was amongst the chief perpetrators of the massacre, killing over twenty defenseless soldiers that day.

The Battle of Bataan Part 1
The siege to April 7th, 1942

By April 7th, the Siege of Bataan reached a critical point for the Allies. The men neared the limit of their resistance with what they had been given. At least the opposition they could give in their current positions.

The Filipino American forces were not at fault for the constant retreat and defeats plaguing Macarthur's forces. The main issue was the simple fact that they had no air and naval support, while the Japanese Army had hundreds of planes to bombard the beleaguered defensive positions in the Peninsula.

The retreat into Bataan (the execution of War Plan Orange-3) had banked on supplies for 40,000 Army personnel, while over 80,000 moved to the area. What was acceptable for defending since more soldiers to man trenches and fire at the enemy was also a problem since American logistical people had moved enough supplies for 40 000 men to last an estimated 180 days (six months). The force being double the planned size made for more consumption. Also, over 20,000 civilians had moved there and consumed food and supplies at an alarming rate.

From the 18th of March 1942, when the battle for the peninsula started in earnest, the struggle became one of attrition. And the simple logic of the mathematics at work did not favor the Allies. They could not be reinforced nor re-supplied by any force, country, or fleet, while their enemy could do so at will with their numerous ships and war supplies. Throughout March, the Japanese received three hundred more planes, two more divisions, several artillery regiments to help with the siege, and tons of ammunition. So what they expanded in terms of ordinance was readily replaced. For the U.S. and Filipino forces, it was not. And the heavier the fighting, the fastest their dwindling reserves disappeared.

By the 7th of April, the battle reached a crescendo that worn-out troops could not sustain. The Allies had established a line that ran west (town of Maudan) to east (city of Maratan) through the Bataan Peninsula. The Japanese pushed hard for several weeks and, on that day, finally broke through in the east at Maratan and outflanked the Allied forces handling the lines at Maudan and Mount Natib. This mountain was deemed impassable by the American High command, so not garrisoned heavily. The Imperial Army used their by-now outstanding and well-demonstrated ability to cross rugged terrain (like they'd done in Malaya and other areas in the Dutch East Indies) and burst into the American-Filipino force's rear.

General Macarthur did not take long to order a full withdrawal southward to save what was left of his command. The outlook was not good for the Allies, and while they were doomed and knew it, they still clung to the last bits of hope that someone would come to the rescue one day.

Two Filipino divisions (the brave 26th recon and the 11th) were encircled entirely and destroyed in Maratan, and the American 7th and 21st Filipino in the west at Maudan. In addition, what was left of the Provisional Tank Force was expanded in a counterattack that enabled the Allied forces to withdraw to a new line of defense southward.

Admiral Nagumo bombs American soil April 7th, 1942

The San Diego Naval base had been important before the loss of Pearl Harbor. While the Oahu port had been the Pacific Fleet home, its conquest by Imperial Japan meant that the US Navy needed a new facility. The 1600 acres of harbor on the Californian Coast fitted the bill perfectly. Its 13 piers, destroyer base, drydock facilities, construction equipment, and protected area for military ships gave it all the prerequisites to be the starting point for the American base for the reconquest. In fact, it was becoming America's most important place for the Pacific War.

The engineers, construction workers, and all manners of military engineering units flocked to the base by mid-March, and several large construction projects were underway. Already, five large airfields were being built just north of the city, while more docks were being added. Shipbuilding facilities were also in the planning stages, and a couple of heavy cruisers were being feverishly finalized in the construction area.

After the loss of Pearl and the Hawaiian Islands, Admiral King, commander-in-chief of the Navy, ordered most of the fleet out of the base in order to await the finalization of the airfields and the arrival of the bulk of the ship transfers. The man wasn't stupid. After getting a bloody nose with a surprise attack on Hawaii, he surmised that a Japanese attack on the

U.S. mainland was a definite possibility. And San Diego would be a prime target.

No less than six battleships, four carriers, and several smaller ships were moving or ordered to move toward San Diego from the Atlantic. The goal was to assemble a powerful fleet with which to sail and challenge the Japs on Oahu. Congress and the Navy had also started or approved new constructions, so hundreds of warships, from the large (carriers, battleships) to the small (escort carriers, destroyers), would soon be a reality.

In the meantime, King had crammed over 500 fighters in the area, from Los Angeles to San Diego and between, with all available airfields and aircraft-suitable areas (flat ground, farm fields). Additional radar stations had been installed along the coast, and a submarine screen sailed over 500 miles from the Californian Coast as an early-warning detection net.

Ten destroyers were positioned around the harbor, with four light cruisers. The fleet also had the California and Tennessee battleships. Their job was to add anti-aircraft firepower to the defenses. Further south on the Mexican coast sailed the Hornet and the Yorktown, two of the fleet carriers that would be based in San Diego soon. But King had decided to sail them far away from danger. Several destroyers and other surface ships escorted them, but they were out of range and out of trouble.

On the morning of the 7th of April, a frantic radio call from the Submarine USS Swordfish announced that a large Japanese fleet had been spotted. The American ship didn't engage but kept a healthy distance from the enemy. Its orders were to shadow the Imperial Fleet and report on its whereabouts.

The Americans waited a couple more hours before launching a large air raid on Nagumo's ships. The Nipponese planes had greater range than their U.S. counterparts, so they had already lifted off their flattops when the sub spotted them. It was thus quickly determined by radar that the Japs had a jump on them and that they already had their planes close to the city. Most of the airstrike was redirected at San Diego's air defense. The base commander only sent a hundred torpedo planes without escorts toward the enemy carrier task force because it was out of range of the P-40 fighters. Over 300 Zero and Val bombers approached the base.

The clash in the air was the biggest in the war to date, the Japanese finally encountering some opposition, and roughly equal numbers of planes slugged it out just above the sea a few miles off the San Diego Harbor. The Imperial pilots were quite experienced and had better planes (the Zero fighter was a much superior machine than the P-40). So, while they incurred some casualties, they exacted a heavy toll on the inexperienced Americans and their inferior aircraft.

At one point, the Val bombers were able to get through the U.S. aircraft screen and made their run over the harbor, which lighted up with flak tracers as they approached. The Nipponese pilots faced real anti-aircraft opposition in the Pacific War for the first time. The powerful and well-coordinated American flak gunnery shot down several planes.

And then the twenty-five remaining Japanese planes could lose their bombs at the ships in the harbor, and ten more also loosed their bombloads at the closest airfield near several of the piers. Finally, five Zeros broke through and flew directly over some of the reserve oil tanks south of the port facilities and strafed them.

The result was not significant for Japan, but still a form of achievement. Two bombs were lodged into the USS California, almost capsizing it, and a light cruiser was sunk. Three hangars and over twenty planes were destroyed on the San Bernardino Airbase. The strafed oil tanks blew up, creating a catastrophic chain explosion in its immediate area, killing over a thousand military and civilian personnel.

By the time the imperial pilots turned tails and raced back to their carriers, the city of San Diego was jutting smoke, the harbor burned, and wreckage from the battle was strewn about everywhere. Planes got shot down, and the pilots from both sides frantically tried to survive in the water.

Japanese losses in the battle were a staggering forty planes (losses they could hardly afford), while the Americans lost over 100 aircraft that could be easily replaced. Also, the U.S. would retrieve most of its downed pilots since they fell into the sea, while the Japanese flyers, at best, were doomed to become prisoners of war. And that was for those with the brains to fly with a parachute, as the habit wasn't common amongst imperial pilots.

About half an hour after the San Diego struggle was over, the hundred or so torpedo bombers (SBD Dauntless) sent by the Americans finally arrived over the Imperial Navy fleet. A small CAP of about twenty Zeros (combat air patrol) flew over the ships and so raced ahead to intercept the enemy. They quickly destroyed several American planes, but their sheer number made several get through the light Japanese screen, so the ships opened up with all their might on their attackers. The sky filled with arcing tracers and dark explosions. More Yankee pilots met their fiery end, hit by the excellent Nipponese gunnery skills honed by several years of war and training.

About thirty of them lined up or dove down for their final run and loosened the bombs under their bellies. Japanese destroyers raced ahead to cover the capital ships, and the rest of the large vessels moved in crisscrossing patterns to avoid the weapons fired at them.

Some of the weapons were bound to hit, so several sirens blared aboard Akagi as two torpedoes were just about to hit the carrier. Everything was done to avoid the American weapons, but the great ship was no nimble destroyer. So, the USA was finally able to score a few hits on an enemy capital ship. Nagumo listened to the watch officer calling the enemy weapons' distance. He braced for impact by tightening his hold on the bridge's metal ramp in front of the large viewport and hoped a miracle would happen.

"100 meters... 50 meters... 25 meters... Brace for impact," yelled the man. The Admiral closed his eyes in desperation and panic. And then, nothing. No explosion. Just a muffled noise. "Report," "Admiral, the bombs missed Akagi my meters and exploded in the water...." The radio officer also reported near misses on other ships. Only destroyer Ghishara had been hit, as was evident by the fact that the boat was on fire and sinking just off starboard from the Akagi. The Kaga had also been missed by several bombs that lifted big water geysers in the sky.

In short, the Japanese got lucky. Hitting a naval ship in a battle was no easy feat, and while the U.S. pilots were full of willingness, their training was lacking.

After the failed American plane attack, Japan was in a good position to launch a second and a third strike and severely damage San Diego harbor. But they didn't send a second wave. Admiral Nagumo's insecurities got the better of him, and he hastily ordered a complete turnaround for Kiddo Butai. Even the sighting of a small aircraft carrier (it was the USS Long Island's task force, cruising 400 miles from the main Jap fleet) did nothing to stir the cautious naval commander to send planes to try and destroy it.

Attack Run

SBD Dauntless over Kido Butai, April 7th, 1942

Dive bombing had a simple way of doing things: You fired from close range to shoot someone. Of course, the closer you got to the enemy, the more likely he would shoot you down. Diving nearly vertically on a ship and releasing the bomb at a low altitude was how you did it. The quickness of the dive also reduced your risk somewhat. Ultimately, dive-bombing was a high-payoff, high-loss activity.

As he sped full speed down toward the giant carrier laid out before his plane, explosions rocked the SBD Dauntless; he was flying. It was sheer madness, and he knew it. He wasn't really trained for dive-bombing. He'd learned the tricks of the trade somewhat in the military academy flight school. But that was it. He'd just been ordered aboard a plane to fly toward the enemy.

Such was the U.S. position these days. Everything, every move, was desperate. Harry had first fought in the dreadful battle over Oahu and eventually fled the Hawaiian Islands on a submarine. He'd ended up sometime later in San Diego and been requisitioned to transfer to Naval Air Station North Island, or NAS North Island, at the Coronado peninsula's north end.

The times were chaotic. Men came from everywhere. Leftovers from the Pacific disasters, transfers from the East Coast, and green pilots directly from the Texas flight schools. Him. Harry Bergman. The General commanding the base had not assigned him to any unit yet when the alarm siren blared. Jap planes were approaching San Diego, and a fleet had been detected westward.

He'd been ordered to get on a plane and follow the flight leader toward the enemy fleet. The aircraft had been hastily armed with its purpose-built 1000-pound bomb and launched into the sky. Initially, he had not been familiar with the controls, but in the end, it was just another aircraft, albeit slower than what he was used to with his P-40 Warhawk.

The flight leader had given them diving instructions over the radio (it was a long flight to their objective, so he had had the time). "Here is how we do a typical dive-bombing attack.", said the man (Bergman didn't remember his name). We will stay at 18,000 feet and fly in a stacked V formation of three for mutual protection. If we're lucky and the air is clear, we'll be able to see 30 to 40 miles and spot the enemy ships.". He paused to take a breath. "Once we spot the target, we all drop down to about 8,000 feet, accelerating as much as possible." The commander had then laughed nervously, hearing total silence on the waves. Most of the pilots in the 100-plane raid toward the Japanese task force had not been trained to do what they were about to attempt. "Look, guys. I know for many of you, it's a first. But the country needs you, and that is that." His word seemed to calm everyone, and the commander felt it over the radio waves.

With silence again, he'd continued: "So we'll attack along the length of the ship to avoid a downrange error, and it'll give more surface to hit. The enemy ships will try to dodge and will certainly pepper the area around your ship with flak. Just keep on a straight dive, and at 2000 feet, drop your bomb. Don't forget to pull on your stick to take altitude afterward. Ah, and I almost forgot. When you climb back up, try to do so in an unpredictable pattern, as the flak will try to hit you on where you will be flying, so throwing off their aim might help you survive."

And such had been Bergman "training on the go" for the attack on the Japanese task force. They'd found it, and most planes went on to dive. Some never made it, their moves and skills too clumsy to get over the enemy ships. As the seconds ticked by and he dove through the dark puffs of smoke from the flak explosion, with tracer shells zipping by his planes and some of his comrades being shot down, he had one last fleeting thought about how ridiculous the situation was. America was employing untrained dive-bomber pilots for the most important strike mission of the war to date. That's what the country was down to. He wondered why the United States was so unprepared for war.

And then came the time to launch his bomb. He pulled hard on the stick and quickly moved it left and right to dodge the oncoming flak. The SBD's engine strained hard, but he reached a safe altitude.

He turned his aircraft back to see the dive bomber's attack result. He found no Japanese ships on fire apart from a small destroyer. Almost everyone had apparently missed. He saw the lines of tracer shells still arcing in the sky from the enemy ships. Several U.S. planes were down on the water, burning or sinking, and he even saw a Zero fighter blaze away at one of his comrades, shredding the left wing, making the American plane spiral down catastrophically in the sea, ending its fall with a big splash.

"Back to base!" blared the commander over the radio. And indeed, without almost any hits or success to their actions, the American pilots turned tails and ran back to base.

Yamashita tries to get the US forces to surrender.

To: General Douglas MacArthur

Commander-in-Chief

United States Army Forces in the Far East

Sir:

You are well aware that you are doomed. The end is near. The question is how long you will be able to resist. You have already cut rations by half. I appreciate the fighting spirit of yourself and your troops, who have been fighting with courage. Your prestige and honor have been upheld. However, to avoid needless bloodshed and save the remnants of your divisions and your auxiliary troops, you are advised to surrender.

In the meantime, we shall continue our offensive, as I do not wish to give you time for a defense. If you decide to comply with our advice, send a mission as soon as possible to our front lines. We shall then cease fire and negotiate an armistice. Failing that, our offensive will be continued with relentless force, which will bring upon you only disaster.

Hoping your wise counsel will so prevail that you will save the lives of your troops, I remain,

Yours very sincerely,

Commander-in-Chief,

The Japanese Expeditionary Force

When I failed to respond, they showered our lines with a leaflet reading:

The outcome of the present combat has already been decided, and you are cornered to oblivion. However, being unable to realize the current situation, blinded General MacArthur stupidly refused our proposal and continues a futile struggle at the cost of your precious lives. Dear Filipino Soldiers! There is still one way left for you. That is to give up all your weapons immediately and surrender to the Japanese force before it is too late; then, we shall fully protect you. We repeat for the last!

Surrender at once and build your new Philippines for and by Filipinos.

Every foxhole on Bataan rocked with ridicule that night. We were just not about to surrender to the damned Japs. Well, at least not before we'd expanded every ounce of our strength.

Our food situation had been increasingly prejudiced by the many civilians who had fled into Bataan with our army forces. The Japanese had craftily furthered this movement by driving the frightened population of the province of Zambales, just north of Bataan, into our lines, knowing full well we would feed them—a humanitarian measure that cut deeply into our food stocks. I had to establish refugee camps back of our defense positions for many thousands of these forlorn people, mostly older men, women, and children. It forced me to cut the soldiers' ration not only in half but later to one-quarter of the prescribed allowance. Ultimately, we were subsisting on less than a thousand calories a day. Everywhere was that poignant prayer, "Give us this day our daily bread." The slow starvation ultimately produced exhaustion, which became the most potent factor in the destruction of the garrison.

Battleship Yamato, April 12th, 1942

Commander Minoru Genda looked intently at the map laid before him by one of Isoroku Yamamoto's staff officers. The Hawaiian Islands depiction was full of drawings and circles covering large areas around the Island chain.

Right beside him, the Grand Admiral was waiting for his reaction. "Commander Genda, what you see here is the first depiction of the coverage we should have with our air fleets with the airfields currently existing or under construction by the Imperial engineers." The commander-in-chief of the Navy looked on his left toward Admiral Nagumo, the recently returned commander of Kiddo Butai after his successful raid on San Diego. However, the attack confirmed what Yamamoto thought about attacks on the American mainland; it was risky, and ground-based planes could attack the ships that had to sail within range of the coast to attack its harbor. The battle had gone Japan's way this time, and thanks to Nagumo's proverbial prudence, the fleet carriers had come back mostly unscathed, apart from some easily repairable damage.

With Nagumo not adding a word, Yamamoto continued. "I have prepared a full depiction of what should be our maximum range for our Zero planes and torpedo bombers when the time comes for the U.S. Navy to come back here and try to take back Oahu from us." "Grand Admiral," bowed Genda respectfully. "Thank you for this map and this plan you are presenting me. How can I help you with it?" For the commander doubted that the Grand Admiral had brought him to the Yamato battleship, in the large commander of the fleet cabin at that, for small talk or to boast about the plan.

"Commander Genda," started Isoroku a little wearily. "Admiral Nagumo and I disagree on when we should send our forces. There are several options here, one of which is to strike from the furthest possible range and thus try to destroy the American fleet before it gets in range. The other is to wait for the enemy to draw closer to the island and then attack.". The Grand Admiral paused and put his fists on the table and the map, resting on it for emphasis. "Option one gives us maximum security and the possibility the enemy might turn around, while option two gives us a better opportunity to destroy the U.S. fleet. It will be difficult to retreat once drawn in, especially if we have the Imperial Navy from Pearl Harbor to sortie and try to intercept them."

Minoru did not have to ask Yamamoto what option he favored or the one preferred by Nagumo. The old, cautious admiral apparently wanted to attack from the safety of the Hawaii Islands air umbrella. In contrast, the Grand Admiral wished to have a go at the complete destruction of the American fleet.

Genda was still sore about the reports from the San Diego raid. Yes, Nagumo saved the fleet by retiring early into the fight, but at the same time, he had lost an opportunity for an airstrike at a lone aircraft carrier. He didn't know what would have been the outcome of such a gamble, but he knew he would have taken the chance.

The ace pilot understood Nagumo's reasons for caution. The Empire could not afford to lose any fleet carrier as it would not be easily replaced.

Its pilots were also a vital commodity to the Navy, so losing too many of them would also be a disaster.

But he sometimes wondered if the cautious Admiral understood the concept that a weapon is to be used in battle, even if one ran the risk of damaging it while fighting. Such was the way of Bushido. A Samurai did not shirk away from a fight because he could get a bloody nose or break his weapon.

"Grand Admiral," he stated confidently, looking sideways at Nagumo's reaction. I do not know which option each of you favors, but I prefer to try and destroy the American fleet if we have the chance and not let the battle happen later." Yamamoto, seemingly quite happy with Genda's answer, continued. "Please explain your reasons."

"It's relatively simple, Your Excellency. You, of all people, know as much as I how much the U.S. industrial infrastructure can produce combat ships, and at which speed it can outpace Japanese military production. I have seen in my recent travels the giant shipyards on the western and eastern coasts of the United States. We all know of their prodigious capability to produce civilian goods and ships. Once this capability is completely switched over to the war economy...." He let the last word hang for a second. "I am afraid that Japan will be buried in steel and might. So we need to strike fast and hard. Perhaps if we sink enough of their ships as they build them, the U.S. President will see the folly of confronting Imperial Japan." He paused to look at Nagumo this time. "We might even win the war if we play our cards correctly."

Apparently satisfied (he harbored a quiet, tiny smile), Yamamoto gave a tap on the table before righting himself up to look at Nagumo. "Chuichi, the matter is thus decided. We will try to get the U.S. Navy to come closer for battle and sink the whole fleet in one battle. We will use our superior firepower while we still have an edge and try to confront the Americans whenever they choose to come to our beautiful Hawaiian Islands."

Nagumo bowed respectfully. "Let it be so, Grand Admiral." "Thank you both for this discussion. You are dismissed." And at that, Yamamoto signaled the two officers that the meeting was over.

Armored belt inspection, April 14th, 1942

Engineer second class Tameo Ishikoga was lowered on the work platform to inspect the outer aft structure of the battleship Yamato. He was on a suspended wooden platform used for ship inspection, repair, and painting. The great ship had recently dueled with large naval guns during the invasion of Hawaii. As such, it had been hit several times on its superstructure by the Diamond Head naval artillery. While none of the hits had destroyed anything vital on deck or penetrated the ship's protection, it was not certain that it had come out of the battle completely unscathed.

The engineer units responsible for the Imperial ship's maintenance had toured the battleship by sailing around it and found several impact marks. From the outside, they looked little more than blackened charcoal spots or as if something fierce had burned and hit the armor.

The fact of the matter was that the Yamato-Class battleship had been designed to be the strongest ship ever built. Japan faced the Western powers (Britain, USA, France) numerical superiority, so the super-ship was constructed in such a way that it was supposed to be able to duel with several large enemies simultaneously and come out a winner.

In order to do so, the Japanese designers had equipped it with the biggest guns and the best optics in the world. So the concept and Imperial Navy hopes were that it could sink anything and penetrate any armor belt of any navies at the time.

But as an unavoidable rule of sea combat, a dreadnought's power was as much based on offensive weapons as its defensive protection. So the Japanese logic had been that they would make its armor so thick that most enemy warships could not penetrate its superstructure or even destroy its guns.

It wasn't difficult to figure it out. At 72,000 tons of armor and might, the ship was built to be the most powerful afloat and dominate its opponents, as numerous as they may be at any given time. Japan's confidence and hopes rested in it just as the carrier age dawned and showed so much promise that it threatened to render the battleship obsolete.

Ishikoga gestured a hand to the seamen above him to stop the platform from lowering. He'd arrived in front of the first impact to be inspected. After careful questioning and a search of the Diamond Head fortress and soldiers that had defended it, it was determined that the Americans had taken Yamato's as one of the main targets and that several 381mm guns had hit it. Tameo was in front of such a hit.

He ran his hand across the smooth but blackened surface. To his pleasant surprise, the armor plate wasn't even buckled or bent. Taking a closer look, he could not even find a crack in the steel or anything that resembled damage. The enemy shell had just exploded, and apart from making a spectacular firework boom, nothing terrible had been sustained by the vessel. Satisfied, he moved on to the next impact they'd marled for inspection on the ship's side.

A few hours later, the engineer happily reported to Grand Admiral Yamamoto that the super-battleship had lived up to its design in its first battle. Besides needing a good clean and a new paint coat, the ship was in perfect combat shape.

CHAPTER 4

Surface action, April 11th, 1942

By early April 1942, The Japanese invasion of the Dutch East Indies progressed quickly as they advanced from their starting points (Palau Islands, Cam Rahn, Tainan Island) and captured bases in Sarawak and Davao in the southern Philippines. They then seized more bases in eastern Borneo and the northern Celebes.

Then, it was time for the killing stroke and land troops on the Island of Java (where the capital of the Dutch East Indies was located), Sumatra, and Southern Borneo. The Imperial Navy thus sailed out with a large number of troops, flanking them with a sizeable force of their powerful destroyers and heavy cruisers just in case the Allies decided to get aggressive.

And they did. Admiral Thomas C. Hart was the commander of a mixed force of Dutch, American, British, and Australian warships that was about to try and stop the Japanese from invading.

The first action was on the 10th of April, when a force of three American destroyers sunk two troop transports as they approached Balikpapan in Borneo. They were driven off by a few well-timed Japanese air attacks. The next morning, the Dutch fought the Battle of Palembang, their flagship heavy cruiser De Ruyter, preventing Japanese forces from capturing the major oil port in eastern Sumatra.

Again, the Allied ship had to retire upon being attacked (unsuccessfully) by Japanese aircraft. Still, the enemy naval attacks had been enough to alert the Japanese high command that something needed to be done to eliminate the Dutch-Australian-British-American naval forces in the area. Japan had not conquered enough airfields close to the Java Sea to solve the problem with their proverbial planes, so they decided to rely on their surface assets, which were none too shabby.

On the 14th of April, as a large convoy headed for Batavia, the Dutch capital for the East Indies, Admiral Takeo Takagi decided to commit his strong surface force to escort them. The land forces included two full divisions (the 55th and the 64th), and it was too much of a risk to send them off with the regular lightship escorts.

So the Imperial Fleet that approached Java on that day was composed of the light aircraft carrier Hosho (that would eventually have no part in the battle), and most importantly of the powerful battleships Yamashiro (35 000 tons), Hyuga (37 000 tons) Ise (37 000 tons) and cruisers Takao, Aoba and ten escorting destroyers to provide for close-in protection to the transport themselves. The big ship's job was to take on anything the Allies chose to send in the landing convoy's way.

Seeing the end if they lost Java and the central island of the East Indies, the combined Allied command or ABDA (Australian, British, Dutch, and American command) decided to commit what it could to intercept the ships with the troops. The fleet that steamed to face the Japanese was composed of three heavy cruisers (British Exeter American Houston and Dutch De Ruyter), five light cruisers, and nine destroyers.

Admiral Thomas Hart (Allied naval commander at Java Sea) knew his force was outgunned, but the Allies only needed to destroy the Japanese transport ships. Hence, it was deemed an acceptable risk to face the Imperial Navy's powerful armada.

The fleets spotted each other in the late afternoon on the 14th of April 1942. Admiral Hart, seeing that he was faced with a heavy concentration of troops transport but, as expected, a lot of warships, decided to take the plunge anyway and try to sink the enemy fleet. Both sides quickly closed to firing range and started to fire at around 16:30. Initially, both the Japanese and the Allied naval forces exhibited poor gunnery and torpedo skills.

Despite her recent refit (with the addition of modern Type-284 gunnery control radar), Exeter's gunfire did not come close to the Japanese ships. At the same time, Houston only managed to achieve a straddle on one of the opposing cruisers (Takao).

The only notable result of the gunnery exchange was Exeter being critically damaged by a hit in the boiler room from a couple of shells from Yamashiro, destroying its central section and making it dead in the water. Battleships Hyuga and Ise finished the job a few minutes later with direct hits to the British ship superstructure that exploded spectacularly, showering the sea around with debris and burning wreckage. No survivors were ever found from the stricken vessel's remains.

All that time, the Allied ships tried to reach the Japanese transports, and while some of the destroyers were eventually able to score some serious hits on a couple of large vessels (they sank an hour later), they were not able to get through the Japanese screen.

The IJN destroyers launched two huge torpedo salvos, 92 in all, and scored several hits on four of the Allied destroyers that were all seriously damaged and then tried to retreat at full speed. The Yamashiro caught with one of them before it got out of range and destroyed it with a spectacular hit aft, obliterating it from existence.

By 18h29, the two remaining Allied heavy cruisers tried to make an almost suicidal charge to break through the enemy transports. Still, Takagi's battleships intervened and straddled the three ships with several mighty salvos that broke Houston in half like a cracked egg and started a severe, uncontrollable fire on De Ruyter. The ship listed heavily, most of its main guns out of action. With Admiral Hart dead and no hope of winning the battle, the remaining officers decided that their struggle was over, and they hoisted the white flag as a sign of surrender.

Only a couple of destroyers were eliminated on the Japanese side, and the battleships sustained some damage, mostly shrugged off by their heavy armor.

The Allied force that limped south was but a shadow of itself. The three cruisers, two light cruisers, and five destroyers were gone. The rest of the ships were all damaged, from light to severe.

While the Japanese Admiral let his ships fire as long as they were in range of the enemy, he didn't pursue the fleeing Allies since his mission was to escort the large transport fleet headed for Java and the battle that would decide the fate of the Dutch East Indies.

White House, April 11th, 1942

The U.S. president rolled up the map swiftly and violently, ripping it partially. Roosevelt was mad. "Remove this freaking thing from my sight!" He'd just learned, via telegram, of the disaster in the Java Sea. The ABDA fleet, composed of Dutch, British, Australian, and US ships, had been almost completely sunk; its remnants were limping southward. Their only luck was that the damned Japs had no genuine air cover in the area, their airfields being too far. The map he'd just destroyed showed the Dutch East Indies, the Philippines, and the current frontlines.

"Admiral King, when will this end!" The American leader was not really happy. The U.S. Navy was constantly getting kicked around by the Japanese, and enough was enough. Macarthur was barely resisting in the Bataan Peninsula in the Philippines, and there was no real hope of relieving him anytime soon. According to the news, Singapore's future was bleak now that the Japs had crossed the Johor Strait in force. Japan conquered everything it wanted in the Dutch East Indies, Hawaii was occupied, they'd even struck the mainland, and now this!

"Mr. President. I am sorry to have to say this, but it's going to get even worse before it gets better." Roosevelt skipped a heartbeat at King's words. "What did you say, Admiral?" the U.S. leader answered in a low, menacing tone. He was mad. It wasn't like him to be like that, and the American

Admiral knew it. The man was a good guy, after all. "I said what I said, Mr. President. You know I am a no-bullshit type of man." He paused, facing a now speechless Roosevelt. "There is no real other way to say this. Japan can do whatever it wants in the Pacific right now. Its fleet is dominant, and its troops are too numerous for our feeble forces in the southeast theater. Hell, their fighters, ships, carriers, battleships are better than ours, for Christ's sake!" It now seemed that King was the angry one. "I hate to cut it to you this way, Mr. President, but there is nothing that we can do about it right now but bide our time, produce ships and war equipment, train more pilots, and raise new divisions. The Axis reigns supreme everywhere."

King's little reality check seemed to soothe Roosevelt, who was now much calmer. "Ernest, please excuse me for this outburst," apologized the President. "I just wish we could have some good news for a change," he finished, sighing heavily.

King, feeling he was on a roll, continued, oblivious to the fact that he was beating on a dead horse; his commander-in-chief was calm now. "Well, Mr. President, I hate to cut it to you again, but our ordeal isn't over. While we've shown the damned Japs that it was not the greatest of ideas to come and challenge us on the West Coast, they will continue to conquer territory in the Pacific without much we'll be able to do about it. I've got it from several sources that they have their sights set on several of the important islands like American Samoa, New Caledonia, New Britain, the Solomons, and the like. Hell, they might even land in Australia for all I know...."

Roosevelt seemed to pick up some energy again. "Admiral. I don't care how. I don't care where. But I do care WHEN." "I am sorry, Mr. President?" King wasn't sure he understood what Franklin Delano had just said. "I want you to do something against the Japs. Something in the now, like tomorrow. Very now."

King seemed taken aback by his leader's sudden aggressiveness and resolve. "Well, Mr. President, maybe in six months we can...." "Ernest, I think you've misunderstood me," started Roosevelt sternly. "We will be attacking the Japanese in Hawaii within a few months, or I will have you relieved of command. We have all those reinforcements coming to the Pacific. Assemble them and attack Oahu." For once, King kept silent. The man was usually caustic and difficult, but he knew when not to push his luck. "And I want a plan and a date about an operation within the week." Roosevelt continued. "Oh, and we've got a couple of battleships in San Diego and the Long Islands carrier somewhere in the Pacific. I want to see them in action." The U.S. President stood, and an aide walked to him to help him on his feet. "Yes, Mr. President." King didn't argue. He liked his leadership approach. And maybe it was time, as Roosevelt said, that they strike back. "I'll be back within a week with a plan."

Roosevelt walked out slowly but turned one last time to face King: "You'd better, Admiral. You'd better."

Extract of Tameichi Hara's book Teikoku Kaigun no Saigo 1967

The Battle of the Java Sea

After the conquest of the rest of the Celebes and some support operations in the conquest of Dutch Borneo with landings at Tarakan and Balikpapan on its eastern coast, I was ordered to transfer to Admiral Takeo Takagi task force to escort the large convoy heading for the attack on the central Dutch island, Java.

It is an interesting battle to talk about since, for one of the rare instances in the war, no planes were involved, and the action was a surface-only affair.

The two fleets met off Surabaya's coast. Admiral Hart, the Allied Admiral in command, had a pretty sizeable fleet that had reasonable chances of seriously damaging the convoy, with three heavy cruisers, five light cruisers, and nine destroyers. The enemy ships managed good maneuvering and boxed us in, while the main fleet under Admiral Takagi (with three battleships and two heavy cruisers) was a hundred and fifty miles behind us because they had been ordered to execute a shore bombardment operation in Tarakan, a day before joining us to act as escorts. The moment was pretty dire as the seventy-one ships in the convoy transported two imperial divisions (the 55th and the 64th).

Japanese overconfidence could have played right into the Allies' hands at this point. The twenty-mile convoy was quite a spectacle. An obvious laxity prevailed in the transports with their ill-trained crews. Many of them emitted huge clouds of black smoke from their funnels. They used their radios in violation of the "no-transmission" orders or failed to observe blackout rules at night. The victory disease, I despaired while sailing beside them, had already started to affect Japanese imperial forces. This attitude would prove our undoing in many future battles against the Americans.

It was fortunate for us that there were no enemy submarines on site, as they would have had one hell of a tally. The sky was blue, the visibility perfect for miles on end, and the moon illuminated the night, making us very easy targets as we snaked our way toward Java with the slow transport ships.

Even with all the advantages of position and numerical superiority, the Allies failed to sink a single Japanese vessel in this encounter. The Admiral in command lost heart and simply turned around to run southward after getting several reports of a large Japanese fleet approaching.

It is hard to comprehend why this Allied commander turned around, and we will never know why because he died a few days later in battle. But one thing was certain, a sense of hopelessness reigned amongst Allied officers at Surabaya and in the whole southeastern theater in general. They saw little or no chance of winning. Even if these ships and men knew they would likely face a showdown soon, they faltered when it mattered most.

And one cannot really blame them. They were confronted almost daily with dismal news of one disaster after the other. The first shock had come after the radio messages about the attack and subsequent invasion of Pearl Harbor, effectively removing the U.S. Navy from the Pacific theater. Then, the sinking of the two heavy cruisers Dorsetshire and Cornwall off Malaya a few weeks earlier had been the second significant blow to their morale. The impending doom in Singapore, the Philippines, and the Japanese advancing ever southward into the Dutch realm finished to give them a sense of foreboding and overall loss that affected their morale.

After Hart's fleet turned around, Admiral Takagi got the message that he was risking too much by taking his own damned time. He radioed us in the convoy to stop and wait for the main task force to arrive and cover them with their big guns. A day later, we resumed sailing toward Java, this time under the protection of the three mighty battlewagons Ise, Hyuga, and Yamashiro. That same day, we met the Allied fleet for the Battle of the Java Sea.

Admiral Hart had finally received his final, fateful orders. ABDA's high command directed him toward our fleet in a last-ditch attempt to stop Imperial forces from landing on Java, thus ending the campaign.

The rest of the battle was a succession of near misses and the enemy trying to get through our escort screen, but we were too strong. Our navy outgunned the Allies by a magnitude rarely seen in the Pacific War. The fact that Hart persevered in trying to reach our transport meant that he approached the battleships and heavy cruisers at very short range, thus ensuring that they would all be hit severely. I think of the brave Allied sailors on those ships to this day. They were worthy of even Japanese praise for their courage and willingness to sacrifice it all for a higher cause. They would all have made great Samurais.

The Japanese offensive in Singapore, April 16th, 1942

Ishiro watched as the clumsy but powerful-looking Type 95 Japanese tank rumbled by. He then followed suit, crouching low, flanked in a long line by his comrades. The Japanese soldiers used armored vehicles for protection against bullets. Allied soldiers fired desperately at the enemy tanks on the other side of the large square they were fighting in, but to no avail. The British had poorly planned before the start of the war and had no armor in Malaya, nor any relevant anti-tank guns in near enough numbers. The IJA thus used their Type 95s to great effect in infantry support, and they were the tilting factor so far in the siege of Singapore.

The tank was fit for the job it was undertaking. The decimated 18th Division had not bled for no reason, as they'd created an opening for the 7th armored brigade to be landed by barges on Singapore island itself.

The Type 95 was a 7.4-ton vehicle that had proved quite adept at jungle fighting and infantry support operations since the start of the war. Three brigades (the Imperial Army entertained eight brigades in the Pacific theater) had been moved to invade Southeast Asia. Two of them had thus been employed in the Malaya and Thailand operations. While utterly incapable of facing other modern tanks and while it would prove relatively weak against American and British armor later in the war, it was particularly suited for the 1942 Japanese sweep through the Pacific and

Asia: lightly armed, with a powerful engine, it was a great shield and mobile firepower unit for the all-conquering Nipponese infantry.

Before southern operations, the Imperial Army had not really contemplated action in the thick Asian jungles, being more or less fixated on the Russians and Chinese. The Type 95s were heavily employed in those areas, with success against China and meeting with disaster in the 1939 border clashes with Soviet Russia at the few battles of Khalkhin Gol in Manchuria).

Yamashita had quickly ordered the transfer of the 7th Brigade through the Johor Strait with the same barge that had brought the 18th after the brave Japanese soldiers had taken a solid foothold on Singapore Island.

The 18th was also reinforced with other units (the elite 5th Division). In contrast, the Allied 2nd Australian brigade and several other Indian units had tried to dislodge the Imperial Army from its beachhead. The fighting had been fierce for the last week, and Tanaka and his comrades held on to dear life. They almost broke and ran, but the Nipponese soldiers' resilience was tremendous, and they held in the face of overwhelming odds.

They did have superior air cover and were supported by Yamashita's artillery units on the other side of the Johor Strait, the narrow band of water that separated the city from the mainland.

The depleted 18th had even expanded on the beachhead in the last two days with the help of the newly arrived Type 95s and had thus progressed inland and were now busy exchanging fire inside the city itself.

Standing orders were pretty simple. Every man needed to continue to push forward as hard as possible. As Tanaka watched a fiercely burning building, he hoped they could do so with the tank's help.

The enemy seemed to have installed some trench system across the town's demolished buildings and scattered fortifications. Singapore was a naval fortress, possessing several spots with bunkers and guns.

"Advance!" was the order yelled by their closest officer. Tanaka's officer was long gone, having received a bullet right in the forehead on the beach after the Johor Strait crossing. Three replacements had also been killed since that time. Tanaka even refused a promotion since he first didn't want to lead men and because officers and NCOs were singled out by the city's numerous sharpshooters and snipers. And besides, he hated all forms of authority in the Army, so he could hardly become part of it.

The machine gun's bullet started to rebound on the slowly lumbering tanks. The metal sparked with flashes as the heavy caliber hit it. But the armor held as it was designed to be impervious to machine gun and rifle fire. The bullets ricocheted everywhere around, and once in a while, a stray one would hit a soldier.

The Type 95s, closely packed together for the best protection for the infantry, continued advancing through the square, rolling over obstacles like they weren't even there. The ricocheting noise got heavier and steadier as they approached the Allied line. Ishiro could even hear the Indian soldiers in front yelling in their incomprehensible tongues.

All the while, their Ha-Go (the name of the Type 95s in Japanese) protector fired their main 37mm guns, lifting dirt, debris, and the trenches themselves. Once in a while, they exploded an enemy position or soldier grouping. They got even luckier when they got a machine-gun nest.

While slowly following the armored machine, Tanaka remembered the attack on Nanking in 1937. It was a weird time to think about such a moment, but it was a soldier's way of keeping his mind off the uncontrollable fear he felt when advancing on the enemy. The city they'd attacked at the time was the capital city of the Nationalist Chinese, and it had resisted much like this one. Japanese soldiers' rage had built up strongly during the siege battle, much like the damned battle they fought to take over the British fortress. The Japanese Army had been merciless then, and he grimly decided that it would probably happen again here. They'd killed and raped for days afterward. He still had nightmares about his horrible actions after that victorious siege, but he knew he would do it again. He just hoped his officers would not order them to bury people alive this time. This was the one thing he did that he could still not accept. Tanaka was a tough soldier and had endured much and was without mercy to his enemy. But that deed on that fateful day in 1937 still haunted him.

He was thrown out of his thoughts by the officers around them calling the charge. The Type 85s and the men behind them had reached the trench line, and it was now time for some good old hand-to-hand combat. Like several of his comrades, he jumped on top of the tank, took aim, fired at an enemy, and then jumped into the bloody melee in front of him, with loud yells of the dreadful "Banzai!"

Singapore would not hold long after the attack. General Percival, the commander-in-chief, was close to accepting surrender from General Yamashita. This last little push by the 7th Armored and the 18th Division would probably do the trick to break what was left of Allied morale.

The Japanese invasion of American Samoa

Imperial forces set foot on Pago-Pago Harbor April 20th, 1942

The chain of Islands known as Samoa had a rich history of being wanted by the World's powers. By the end of the 19th century, it was in the middle of intense international tensions between Britain, Germany, and the USA. In the end, Germany got the Western part of Samoa and the United States the eastern part and the island with the biggest potential for a harbor. After the First World War, Germany lost its territory, and it was given by mandate to the United States.

After that, the Americans were free to develop it as a naval base. It didn't take a genius to see the strategic importance of Samoa. It had a great location halfway between the Hawaiian Islands and Australia. The power that controlled it also controlled the sea lanes going to the Sub-Continent.

Following the conquest, the U.S. Navy built a base on the small Island (Tutuila) that housed Pago-Pago. In 1940 it was only a minor naval station lacking the necessary facilities to handle large wartime fleets and logistical needs. As tensions rose with Imperial Japan, the Americans fed more funds into the area, started to work on the harbor facilities, and prepared some defenses. But the money was not enough to make it in a large base, and in the end, American preparations just worked into Nipponese designs.

Nonetheless, it became a high-priority target in Yamamoto's grand strategic plan for dominance in the Pacific. After the fall of Oahu and the rest of the Hawaiian Islands, the U.S. Navy was left with no major port to re-supply its ships on their way to Australia or to wage any type of naval campaign in the Pacific. The Samoan islands were an essential link in the chain of communications between the United States, Australia, and New Zealand. This sea lane also ran through the Fiji islands.

Holding the line drawn from Midway to Samoa and the Fijis was considered essential for the Japanese Grand Admiral. The conquest of these bits of land would effectively cut off communications between the United States and Australia's west coast and help fend off any American naval offensive.

Yamamoto's reasoning was thus simple. Japan needed to take Samoa to keep the USA out of the theater of operation. And it would have the best chance of doing so while it still had numerical superiority. From the moment Oahu was conquered, the rest of Yamamoto's plans to conquer the Pacific Islands were put into motion. Wake Island, Midway Island, Guam, and Johnson Island were rapidly occupied as they were in short range of invading Japanese fleets.

The Gilbert Islands were also within easy reach of the Marshalls, so again were quickly occupied by the end of March. New Britain, Samoa, Fiji, New Hebrides, and the Solomon Islands were next on the list.

A small but appreciable Japanese fleet thus set out from Truk by the end of March and sailed with all due speed toward Samoa. The task force wasn't large by any standards. It didn't need to be because no Allied fleet of any significance sailed the Pacific after Pearl Harbor. So, with seven destroyers, three light cruisers, and five large transport ships, the Imperial Navy brought a whole regiment of Sasebo elite Marines to Samoa. Per usual Imperial Navy doctrine, they landed in total darkness between the 19th and 20th of April, catching the under-strength American battalion defending Pago-Pago totally by surprise.

The Nippon soldiers relied on surprise, their ship's shore-bombardment support, and willpower to assault the American positions without any air cover. The plan worked to perfection, as the U.S. commander on site did not expect an attack so deep into the Pacific.

Also, American soldiers were under-equipped and lacked heavy weaponry, so they were quickly overwhelmed by the experienced Marine regiment that had seen much fighting in China since 1937. The battle didn't even last a full day. On sundown on the 20th of April, the imperial flag was hoisted on Tutuila and Pago-Pago.

Japan held the first strategic Island in its plan to cut all communication between North America and Australia. A few days later, another ship arrived on the island and disgorged imperial engineers, who promptly worked on making a small airstrip for the follow-up convoy scheduled in a few weeks that would include Japanese planes.

The Fall of Singapore

The British surrender, April 17th, 1942

British General Arthur Percival would not go down as one of history's greatest commanders. At the start of the Malayan campaign, he'd enjoyed a comfortable numerical superiority with close to 90,000 troops, while the Japanese never even reached half that number.

It was a typical case of the big army being outmaneuvered by the smaller, nimbler one. The Japanese commander, General Yamashita, led his forces brilliantly. He outflanked the Allies with landings in Kota Bahru and trashed opposition in battles like Jitra, three times superior to his forces.

The Imperial Army forces were also equipped with two very handy armored brigades, while the British had none to oppose them. The Japanese also enjoyed complete air superiority, as shown by the many airstrikes and the sinking of the two heavy cruisers near the Malayan coast at the beginning of the campaign.

In retrospect, the Japanese had been well-led, well-equipped, had planned brilliantly, and faced half-defeated forces in front of them.

As Percival walked the distance between the no-mans-lands between the Japanese positions and what was left of his city's forces holding on to dear life in their trenches, he wondered how he could have lost such a campaign so fast. He was about to surrender the mightiest British fortress. The place was deemed invincible before the war. It boasted significant defensive works and many naval guns, but there had been one problem. An attack had always been expected from the sea. The IJA had attacked from the Malayan Peninsula, crossing jungle terrain deemed impassable by most serious Allied strategists.

Yamashita's offer for surrender had come at midday after the heavy battles of the 16th and 17th of April that had seen several units obliterated and many parts of the city occupied. The Japanese commander had given him sixty minutes to answer, or the imperial soldiers would continue to attack and kill every one of his soldiers.

He'd had to decide Britain's fate in the Far East in less than sixty minutes and in less than an hour. That was not much time to decide something so momentous, so serious of consequences for the British Empire. The loss of Singapore meant the total collapse of British rule in the theater. It meant that it gave the enemy a clear road to sail through the Malacca Strait and pour into the Indian Ocean to attack India. It meant it would free up more Japanese troops to continue pushing through the Dutch East Indies, Burma, and Australia.

And yet, there wasn't much choice. Singapore was encircled, out of supply, and without hope of relief from the faraway Allies. The Americans, at least the closest ones, were also encircled in the Philippines and were fighting a losing battle in the Bataan Peninsula, while the Dutch had their hands full with the Japanese invading their territory everywhere.

Japanese planes ruled the skies, and all the Allied ships were sunk. No fleet could challenge the Imperial Navy in the theater, and General Yamashita held all the cards on land. It was a lost cause.

Victory was no longer the question, nor any possibility of a prologued siege to wait for a relief force. The opposite choice, death, would have meant the useless slaughter of civilians and the brave soldiers who fought since the start of the campaign.

He went, as directed, to the (destroyed) Ford Motor plant at the foot of Bukit Timah, a hill where, earlier that day, there had been bloody fighting. He was escorted by a couple of Japanese officers and followed by his own people to the meeting.

There, at 7 p.m., after some light discussion with a triumphant, arrogant Yamashita, he signed away large pieces of the land, the power, and the pride of the British Empire.

Japan reigned supreme in the southeast.

Office of the British Prime Minister, April 18th, 1942

Old warhorse Winston Churchill took the news of Singapore's fall as he had for the other disasters that had befallen the Empire. First, discouragement and despair, then his characteristic fighting spirit took over again.

He was standing up in his hotel room on the last floor, in one of the suites of the Chateau Frontenac in the Dominion of Canada, the home of the British Empire leadership since the fall of the United Kingdom. He faced the large window that gave him a view of the St-Lawrence River and all the naval traffic steaming it.

"Now, the enemy will come for Australia and India," he thought somberly. Several discussions would need to be had with Imperial Command about it. They could not lose Australia and India, for it would mean the end of the Empire. It would mean giving the damned Japs too many resources and power. The Americans were powerful, but he wasn't confident they could successfully wage war frontally in the Pacific if no one from other fronts helped them.

He turned around, walked a small distance, and stopped by a small table. He picked up a Scotch bottle and poured himself a glass. He then fished a new cigar out of his front pocket and lit it eagerly. He walked back to the window with both in his hands to think.

One thing was sure. India needed to hold. From the reports he'd read, the Indian Subcontinent had a lot of troops and was gearing up to raise more. Their problem wasn't men; it was training and equipment. He resolved to talk to the Americans about it. Sending resources to India and Australia would be complicated and very time-consuming now that they would have to circumvent the Pacific or go around Africa and through the Indian Ocean, but there was no real choice; it had to be organized.

The Invasion of Java and the Fall of Batavia **Japanese Imperial forces takeover Batavia, April 12-16th, 1942**

Batavia was the capital of the Dutch East Indies and the seat of the colonial administration since the 1700s. It was on the north coast of Java, in a sheltered bay, on a land of marshland and hills crisscrossed with canals. It was a very convenient city to run a sprawling colony like the East Indies during peacetime. But against the invading Japanese, it was dangerously exposed. It would not hold long, facing Japan's onslaughts coming from the sea.

By April 12, the Dutch East Indies were in complete disarray. Japanese forces were mopping up the last units in Borneo and controlled most of the main cities. The Nipponese had also landed in southern Sumatra and conquered its major cities in resource-rich areas. The Celebes were also occupied. What was left was a handful of important islands in the east, like Timor and Ambon. And then there was Java. The most critical and best-defended island in all of the Dutch East Indies. The Allies consequently put their last hopes in the battle about to unfold. The Dutch had assembled most of their forces near the capital to execute one final battle and try to reverse the Samurai tide sweeping everywhere in the colony.

The Allied order of battle consisted of three well-equipped Dutch Divisions (mainly of native Indonesians), a British brigade, an American battalion, and an Australian regiment. Unfortunately for the Allied cause, they were not well trained.

The experienced, hardened men of the 14th Army were facing them, coming off of four long years of war in the Chinese theater. The soldiers were well-trained, well-equipped, and led by determined commanders. Their forces included the 2nd, 55th, and 64th divisions, some of the best in the entire Japanese military. And then the last unit was its most fearsome—the Imperial Guard Division. Fifteen thousand strong, with the best equipment (including Type 95 tanks), double artillery compared to standard Japanese units, and the best men the country could offer: A posting to the Guards Division was a reward and a promotion, so the unit tended to gather all the best from the Army into one unit.

Flush from their total victory at the Battle of the Java Sea the day before, the Japanese troops landed at three points on Java on the 12th of April. All their chosen areas were within a maximum of half a day's distance from Batavia proper. Contrary to their normal doctrine, the Imperial Navy operated its amphibious attacks during the day, as everything the Japanese had in the theater was brought to bear: two small aircraft carriers, over eighty Zero fighters flown from the recently operational Tarakan airbase in Central Borneo, four battleships (Tosa, Tamashiro, Ise, Hyuga) and dozens of smaller units.

The Allies tried to oppose the main landing just west of Batavia Bay and were initially able to score some successes in pinning the invaders on the beach and inflicting on them important casualties. But the big guns of the Imperial Navy were called to the scene, and the Allies evacuated under a rain of shellfire. The Japanese forces eventually mastered all three landing points and gathered to push on Batavia.

The Allied commander, Dutch General Hein ter Poorten, opted for a defense directly in the city. After all, his troops had used the better part of the month before the invasion to build trenches and other fortifications, so it was the best way of defending the Dutch capital.

Undeterred, the Japanese forces plunged into battle and fought fiercely as their brothers had in Singapore. For the better part of four days, a bitter battle was fought by both sides. Still, slowly, the Nipponese forces took precedence because they had more soldiers, more guns (their navy), and countless more planes after they destroyed what was left of the Allied air power in the theater in a large dogfight (the biggest of the war to date) over Batavia on the first day of the invasion.

Ter Poorten eventually gave up the fight for Batavia and ordered his troops to retreat south and east to continue the battle. The Dutch were doomed, but it seemed that they had not realized it yet.

On the eve of the 16th of April, the imperial flag was hoisted in the Dutch capital. Japan was almost done with its conquest of the Dutch East Indies.

Dogfight over Batavia

Last call of the Dutch Royal Airforce April 12th, 1942

Takeshi Onishi and thirty of his Zero comrades had been ordered to fly cover for the landings near Batavia on the 12th of April. Their bases were quite far, and they couldn't intervene on a dime. It prevented the Air Force from participating in the Battle of the Java Sea the day before.

But they could do it with a stationary target and the time they needed to be there. The Zero fighter had an incredible range, so it was pretty easy for the Nipponese pilots to get there from their new Tarakan airfield in Central Borneo.

Onishi had been intrigued by the reports of enemy air concentration over the Dutch capital. He longed for a real dogfight and hoped the enemy would be a little more worthy this time than he'd faced to date.

By the time their airstrike arrived over the Javanese coast, Takashi was startled by the sight that greeted them: over sixty fighters were assembled and waiting for them. The Japanese pilots didn't know it, but they had more going for them than appearance showed. Yes, they were outnumbered, but the Allied armada included thirty outdated Dutch P-36s, another twenty again outdated Brewster Buffalos, and a paltry eighteen P-40 Warhawks.

Still, the defenders were stacked in at three levels at least 10 000 feet above the city and a bit higher than the Japanese force, giving them the advantage of altitude.

The Dutch and their allies had assembled every fighter they could find for the decisive battle through superhuman effort and a lot of willpower. And this time, they were warned of the enemy's arrival. This time, they believed that things would be different. This time, they had the numbers and the determination to defend their city.

But they didn't last ten minutes.

It was the biggest air battle in the southeast campaign to that point of the war, and Takashi had a field day. He started with a fast roll on his right and poured a ton of tracers into a slow-moving and clumsy Brewster fighter, shredding it and setting it afire. The Japanese Zeros were so superior to most of their enemies that it seemed they were dancing around them. The training discrepancy was also incredible, to the point that Onishi, shooting down his second plane that day (a P-36), decided that it was borderline criminal to send such untrained men up in the sky against veterans like him and his comrades.

On his fourth kill of the day (a nice P-40 Warhawk), he decided it was beneath him to feel bad for such pilots. They were not worthy of fighting against Japan and deserved to die.

When the biggest air battle of the Pacific war was over, Onishi and his comrades had shot down over forty aircraft, so Allied airpower on Java and the whole of the Dutch East Indies was destroyed.

As he flew back to Tarakan half an hour later (after expending the rest of his ammunition strafing enemy positions to help the Army in their attack), Takashi wondered where he would go next. He wasn't worried; it was more curiosity because the Allies had not shown any capacity to kill him or his brothers so far.

Taskforce Long Island raids the Japs, April 26th, 1942

USS Long Island (CVE-1) was the lead ship of her class and the first escort carrier of the United States Navy. It was originally intended as a large transport ship, but along the way, the U.S. Navy decided that it was to be converted into a small aircraft carrier. It was thus completed with a flight deck with an additional storage area and commissioned on 2 June 1941 as Long Island.

The goal for the ship was to experiment with the possibility of making several smaller (and less costly) carriers from large cargo ships. At first, the project did not pick up a lot of interest in high places, but as tension rose steadily with Japan and war with Germany, the project was given a new life. The ship spent most of 1941 in the Atlantic and escorted troops bound for North Africa and the Agadir front.

By February 1942, it was transferred to the Pacific, and by the time of the attack on Pearl Harbor, it was cruising the shipping lanes near the Mexican coast.

After the Java Sea Battle disaster, President Roosevelt gave a good drubbing to Admiral King for it; then, he tasked the Navy Commander-in-Chief to mount an operation to strike back at the Japanese. Both men knew that the Navy wasn't ready to face the Japanese in open battle since most of the ship transfers from the Atlantic to the

Pacific were still happening at that time, so it was decided to have some modest objectives. The U.S. leadership also had to consider the possibility that Nagumo's carriers could return to attack San Diego.

So the Long Island was ordered to rendezvous with a task force centered around the battleship Tennessee, three heavy cruisers (Vincennes, Wichita, Pensacola), plus eight Destroyers for submarine protection. Their objective was the recently Japanese-conquered atoll of Palmyra, several thousand miles south of the Hawaiian Islands. According to sub recon (the USS Wahoo had been there ten days prior and reported the enemy strength), the Japanese presence represented a minimal risk for the Americans: probably half a battalion, a destroyer, and a seaplane tender.

The American task force did not include foot soldiers or Marines, as its job was only to attack, strike, and then retreat as fast as possible.

It sailed from its rendezvous point a thousand miles off the Mexican coast toward Palmyra, observing total radio silence. After four days of sailing without incident, the task force approached the island.

Palmyra was part of Yamamoto's perimeter defense strategy that he wanted to install across all of the Pacific. The goal was to have fortified islands across the expanse in order to block the Allies from penetrating it too deeply. Places like Palmyra were thus supposed to have airfields built, a small naval squadron, and some submarines to defend them. Yamamoto then envisioned the Combined Fleet to intervene at any given point once the Americans were spotted.

The tiny atoll had just been conquered by a small force of Japanese Marines that landed there at the beginning of April. Conquered was a big word for the deed. Yes, the men of the 12th Sasebo Special Landing Force (12th SNLF) had hoisted the Imperial flag over the tropical paradise but hadn't encountered any opposition. Apart from a few police officers, the island was empty of people with guns, so they took over.

The Japanese Palmyra defense force comprised 556 men, destroyer Kumaniro, and seaplane tender Sanuki Maru. By no means a threatening force, it had been deemed sufficient for the time being since Yamamoto and his staff believed the US had other fish to fry and would take some time to recuperate from their Pearl Harbor disaster. The force's job was to trigger an alarm if the enemy came by this route.

The Sanuki Maru's job as a tender was reconnaissance. These ships weren't built for the attack but had six to ten large seaplane tenders that could drop into the ocean to fly long-range missions to spot the enemy. The aircraft would take off by themselves, and the ship's job was to take care of them (repairs, gasoline, pilot rest) when they came back and landed beside it on the water with their large floater. They could eventually be hoisted back on the ship with the tender's big crane.

On that lovely morning of the 26th of April, the twelve planes from Long Island seemingly appeared out of thin air over the Palmyra sky and dove down on the Sanuki Maru. Large water geysers soon straddled the ship while the sailors on the destroyers ran to their flak guns and started to fire at the enemy, sending their tracers in long, arcing lines of red shells at the attackers.

The attack ended without any scratch on the Japanese ships, and a few bombs landed on the Atoll itself, killing a few threes. The commanding Japanese officer on the island reported via radio to Pearl Harbor that they'd just been attacked by a small force of American planes and that all was fine. He also ordered the six seaplanes to fly away and find the enemy. Half an hour after the aircraft left, frantic radio calls returned to Palmyra warning of impending disaster. A large fleet was approaching the island. The destroyer immediately picked up steam and raced toward the approaching fleet. The Sanuki Maru also started on its way, but in the opposite direction, to flee the scene.

A new American strike appeared over the Island within another ten minutes, just as the seaplane tender left the atoll. This time, the U.S. aviators came with torpedoes under their bellies and launched at the Japanese ships. Two weapons connected, and while only one exploded on impact, it was enough to stop the Sanuki Maru dead in the water. The hit destroyed the ship's engines.

The brave Kumaniro sailed under full power toward what had been reported as a lone small aircraft carrier raider, fully intent on sinking it. Instead of finding a lone defenseless ship, it fell under the big 356 mm guns of the battleship USS Tennessee. The American dreadnought's first salvo straddled the poor destroyer. Its captain decided that flight was his best option and turned away as fast as possible. But the next U.S. big guns salvo hit the tiny ship right on top of its deck, obliterating it from existence in an instant.

From there, the three American cruisers, much faster than Tennessee, sailed ahead toward Palmyra and arrived within range of the still-stricken Sanuki Maru within an hour. They quickly gunned it down from short range with their 200mm cannons. After the first three salvos, the Japanese ship exploded, receiving well over fifteen direct hits.

The rest of the story was not pretty for the poor Japanese garrison. The Allied gunships shore-bombarded their position for the better part of the day, after which they sailed back toward the eastern horizon.

The Americans left behind a wake of death, a burning island, and a stricken force. But the most important of all was they'd given a message to the Japs that the war was far from over.

USS Wahoo Surface at Samoa, April 29th, 1942

"Something's wrong, captain," said the radio operator to skipper Jim Cloutier. The man he talked to stood beside him in the sub's small, cramped radio room. It was full of radio equipment, and the place had enough space for a small chair and a typewriter for messages or reports. The operator had his headset in his right hand glued to his right ear. "Explain, sailor Harrison," said a curious lieutenant commander. "Well, captain, we've got this Japanese radio traffic, and I am receiving it as clear as day, almost like the transmitter was very close." "Thank you, sailor," finished Cloutier, tapping the man on the shoulder in small praise. "Keep listening and let me know if you end up hearing Pago-Pago Harbor." "Yes, captain," answered the radio operator.

Cloutier opened the small door to the room at the aft end of the control room and walked the distance to the bridge, curving and twisting around since a submarine was no battleship and it was cramped to the extreme.

The ship's bridge was not a big place either. It compressed six people together in a confined space. The two torpedo operators, the captain, the 1st officer, the steering wheel (driver), and the plotting specialist. Arriving on the scene, he gestured to the 1st officer to prepare for a dive. A quick alarm sounded across the ships, and all hatches were closed, especially the one above the bridge that had been opened to let some fresh tropical air in.

The Wahoo was sliding on the gentle Pacific waves, and it was night on the surface, with dawn about to break any moment. Cloutier thought telling everyone on the bridge his intentions were a good idea. "The radio room cannot pick up any American signal coming from Samoa. But it does pick up some Japanese traffic. I do not know what's happening, maybe atmospheric interference or that Pago Pago's radio is defective, but we'll take no chance and approach submerged." After listening, every man returned to their duties, seemingly concerned but concentrating on their post.

Cloutier approached the man at the helm and told him to sail slowly. There really was no rush, and they'd had their share of surprises so far in the campaign. After their stunt near Kwajalein, where they'd sunk a transport ship and avoided Jap destroyers. They then sailed to Palmyra to replenish their supplies and see if they would find a stray Japanese vessel or two. To their astonishment, the enemy occupied the atoll, which appeared to be a destroyer and a seaplane tender. With the latter being well protected in the atoll's lagoon and with the presence of a destroyer, Cloutier had decided that it wasn't worth the risk and had turned around, sailing away. But he still reported Japanese presence to Navy Command, which in turn helped the Americans mount their Palmyra operation on April 26th.

Then they'd set sail for Samoa, where the lieutenant commander hoped to get some RR time (rest and refit) for his men to walk on firm ground, get some decent food, and the likes. On the way, they'd had a scuffle with a long-range Japanese seaplane that tried to take a shot at them with a bomb but missed, and they'd just dove to avoid a return pass. The damned Jap planes had appeared out of nowhere while the Wahoo had been sailing topside (on the surface). Then, they'd shadowed a sizeable Japanese convoy that seemed to be headed in the general direction of the Carolinas or somewhere in the Central Pacific. The force boasted over ten destroyers and a giant capital ship, including aircraft carriers. Again, he relayed the position and followed the enemy fleet for a few days before breaking off, having received strict orders not to engage. The high command wanted him to continue to sail on toward Australia.

And so they were finally approaching Samoa, his intended destination. But now, Cloutier wasn't so sure that they would be able to go to land. He took a mental note to go and see the supply officer to discuss how long they still had in terms of fuel, food, and other necessities. If the Wahoo couldn't resupply in Samoa, they would have to find a place because he wasn't sure they had what they needed for the cruise to Australia. Typically, a Gato-Class submarine had enough fuel for a 75-day cruise, but they hadn't started the war at full gauge, and he didn't even have his usual complement of torpedoes.

As he dwelled in his thoughts, the submarine completed its dive. The crew droned the standard routine orders and discussions while the sub was submerged. They were about an hour away from the Island of Tutuila, where the harbor was located.

An hour later, they were in the visual range of Pago-Pago harbor. Cloutier picked up the range-finding periscope (there were actually two periscopes in each Gato-Class submarine, one for range-finding and one for combat) and pushed it up, "Periscope up," said Cloutier. He turned it toward the island, holding it with two small convenient handles that enabled him to control the large piece of equipment. "Damn." What he saw was the unmistakable proof of enemy presence in Samoa. He had a large Japanese Imperial flag towering above the harbor and a few destroyers, also of Japanese designs, cruising in and out of the place. There were even a few planes flying overhead (seaplanes). Fearing detection, he dropped the periscope right away. "The enemy occupies Tutuila and Pago-Pago," he said gravely. He sensed the discouragement from the men around him. Everyone, including Cloutier himself, had been looking for some downtime on firm land.

He took a few more seconds to digest the bad news and returned to his senses. "Well, gentlemen, we're at war. These things happen." He gestured to the 1st officer. "Get me the internal radio. I need to talk to the crew."

A few seconds later, he announced to the Wahoo's men that there wouldn't be any stop in Samoa. "I understand everyone's disappointment, but I'll be damned if we let the Japs get away with wiping out our vacation plans. We'll find some plum target and sink it, leave this place, and head for Australia as ordered. Captain out." The crew cheered at their skipper's words.

New Britain, Solomon Islands, and New Guinea, Apr-May 1942

Truk Lagoon was an island in the middle of the Carolina Islands chain, forming a rough triangle of more than thirty miles on each side. Inside the lagoon were many islands, of which more than eight were more than one square mile in size.

It provided the Japanese with sufficient anchorage for a whole Japanese battle fleet during the war and enough space to allow several vessels to maneuver for training, all in the protection of the lagoon itself. The many islands also provided enough room for several airfields.

When Japan occupied the area in World War One, the Imperial Japanese Navy quickly recognized its importance for controlling the southwest Pacific and the eventual conquest that would inevitably follow if Japan wanted to expand.

The importance of the Truk atoll in the Carolinas grew at the war's start since Tokyo planned to form a defensive perimeter to the east of the Mariana's line into the Gilberts, Ellice, New Caledonia, and the Marshall Islands. Truk occupied a crucial position in the middle Pacific area, able to control Midway to the north, the Marshalls in the East, and Rabaul and New Britain to the south. It could also be the supply area for any campaigns in the Solomon Islands and beyond, such as cutting Australia's communication and supply lines.

So, the Truk base was the perfect stepping stone for the Japanese invasion of the Islands and territories bordering the Coral Sea. Yamamoto aimed to occupy everything from New Guinea, the Solomons, to the New Hebrides and Fijis. He wanted to form an encirclement ring against Australia to deny the shipping lanes to the Allies. It would also force his enemies to retake the remote islands by force if they wanted to do anything about it.

Beyond that, the hotheads in the Army also wanted to have a shot in Australia. Yamamoto was totally against it, but the IJA had pretty much decided it would attack the Aussies via Darwin. Hence, the Grand Admiral agreed to make the best out of a bad situation and help the Army put a stranglehold on Oceania.

The Grand Admiral transferred several strong ships to the area to make his invasion plans work, centered around main fleet carriers Soryu, Hiryu, and light carriers Zhuiho and Ryujo. A powerful surface force would supplement them with the two fast battleships Haruna and Kongo, with three heavy cruisers, six light cruisers, and fifteen destroyers.

The ships would be responsible for escorting and executing several amphibious landing operations with the numerous forces that the Imperial Army had accepted to lend for the attack.

The complex operation had several critical objectives. First and foremost, it would start with a landing in the Australian-held territory of New Britain, and more specifically at the city of Rabaul, which had all the prerequisites to be made into a significant base. The Imperial Navy indeed envisioned the town to be built into a substantial supply and command area responsible for controlling the Coral Sea theater.

Once this first stepping stone was accomplished, the Imperial Navy would fan out onto different islands, starting with Guadalcanal (Solomon Islands). Yamamoto wanted a large airfield built there to control shipping in the area and as a relay to fly aircraft to New Caledonia.

Once Imperial army forces mastered the whole of New Britain, the 67th Division would make landfall in northern New Guinea and take control of the small villages of Lae, Guna, and Buna. The goal was to prepare the final attack on the southern coast against the major Australian base of Port Moresby. Controlling eastern New Guinea would ensure Japanese dominance in the theater and prevent the Aussies from doing anything against Rabaul.

By April 26h, the large fleet, including over seventy-three troops' transports, left the protected Truk Lagoon and headed for Rabaul, sailing at fifteen knots to keep pace with the slow troop carriers.

Early on the 27th, the four Japanese carriers got in range of Rabaul and launched a devastating airstrike on the Australian base, smashing the airfield and destroying most planes (there were only a

few anyway) on the ground. The base was lightly defended by a battalion and very few other defenses apart from some flak cannons. In 1942, Australia was not yet a military force to be reckoned with. Besides, the country had sent several units to the European war to help the United Kingdom, so it was caught with its pants down when the Japanese attacked.

The country's strategy was thus to defend Australia properly since they didn't have the necessary troops (and no outside Allied help) to handle their exterior defense line. The military still decided to make a good defense of the Port Moresby base, but it just didn't have a lot of troops to spare if it wanted to prepare for a potential Japanese invasion of their continent.

By the 28th of April, the main fleet approached Rabaul, and the troops landed without much opposition. The 44th Regiment took hold of the beaches without a hitch and quickly consolidated its beachhead, while more strikes and shore-bombardment operations were executed against the force defending Rabaul proper. The New Britain Allied commander opted to stay entrenched in Rabaul and fight as best he could against the oncoming enemy onslaught.

But it didn't take long for the few Australian forces to be overwhelmed and outfought. The Japs just came at them too hard and with too much superiority for them to resist long. On the 30th of April, following an ultimatum from the 44th commander, the Australians agreed to surrender and hand over control of Rabaul to the Japanese.

The first of many dominos had just fallen, and there was not much in the way of Yamamoto's grand designs.

USS Wahoo attacks Japanese shipping in Samoa April 30th, 1942
Lieutenant-Commander Jim Cloutier gave one last look at the fat-looking Japanese transport that was slowly entering the harbor before giving the order to fire a couple of torpedoes. "Forward torpedoes fire," he gestured, pointing backward with his finger (the torpedo firing mechanism was behind the periscope, and its operator faced Cloutier's back.)

The USS Wahoo had been waiting for the last day, anticipating a nice target. The ship was nicely lined up perpendicular to the Pago-Pago harbor's entrance. For a moment, Cloutier had wondered if anything would show up since he couldn't stay in Samoa forever with his dwindling supplies.

And then, half an hour ago, the Japanese transport ship had shown up. The thing seemed full of supplies and had some planes on its decks, also filled with crates. He'd waited patiently for the vessel to enter the Wahoo's sights. A couple of destroyers were close, keeping watch and trying to cover the angles, but overall, he thought Japanese security was relatively lax like it had been in Kwajalein.

The four Mark 94 torpedoes (the sub had six forward tubes for launching its weapons) went straight for the target. It was apparent that the Japs had seen their wake as the ship seemed to scramble for speed. He also saw the two destroyer's funnel gushing forth with dark smoke, a sure sign that they were picking up speed – and coming his way.

He watched for the few more seconds it took for the four torpedoes to reach the target. The Japanese convoy ship could not dodge, and the American ordnance impacted the ship. Only one of the Mark 94s exploded. It did so right in the middle of the boat, lifting it from the sea in two pieces, catastrophically opening it to water and igniting a gigantic explosion. The Nippon ship was, unknown to Cloutier, full of ammunition and plane gasoline. So its destruction was more spectacular than any he'd seen. Secondary explosions, even more potent than the first one created by the torpedo, scattered horizontal and vertical pillars of fire and dark smoke that gushed forth in a starlike pattern, showering debris and shrapnel all around. One of the destroyers was caught by the blast and disappeared from Jim's view. Again unknown to Cloutier, already busy giving the dive orders (time was of the essence now since the enemy ships would try to locate them and send depth charges to kill the Wahoo), the Jap ship was heavily damaged. It would have to be returned to Japan for major repairs the day after the attack.

The submarine went as deep as possible (it was a shallow sea around Samoa) and pushed its engine to the maximum. While the turtle-like nine knots the Gato class could make while submerged underwater, it was what Cloutier had at the moment. He wanted to put as much distance as he could with the Japanese destroyer that came right for them the last time, he looked in the periscope that was now down since the vessel was underwater and speeding up.

They'd spotted a deeper area north of Tutuila Island and wanted to make it there to put more distance between the Wahoo and the enemy hunter.

The Japanese ship was on to them, and they could even hear the ping noise of its sonar. "Keep pushing the engine!" yelled the 1st officer on the internal radio to the engine room.

After a ten-minute chase, the Japanese destroyer was over them, and everyone in the Wahoo could hear its ignominious propeller battering the sea above. And then loud thuds could be heard by the listening sailor. "Depth charges in the water!" "Everyone, brace for impact!" yelled the 1st officer yelled on the internal radio.

And then their world rocked. Three loud booming noises were heard, and the Wahoo shook from all its length. Every sailor or officer who hadn't held on to something solid was thrown out of their feet, falling on the ground or hitting walls. Several injuries would later be reported.

"Release oil, all stop to the engine, sink to the bottom!" yelled Cloutier through the hatch, without waiting for the 1st officer to relay his order. The move was a typical submariner's trick they learned in training. It was intended to fool the enemy into thinking it sunk their ship. Stopping the engine dead and sinking to the bottom also signaled the enemy they were done for.

A tense minute passed while the Japanese destroyers circled around for another pass at where they were. In the meantime, the sub had dropped all the way down on the seafloor, where it rested. "More depth charges into the water!" yelled the sailor at the listening station. And then their world shook again, but less violently, this time since they were already on the seafloor, and they'd been lucky to land on a sand bed.

Everyone stayed still for a few minutes while the Japanese ship circled again to return to its position. The hunter dropped two more depth charges for good measure and then sailed back toward Pago-Pago to help their stricken comrades and try to salvage the disaster that had befallen them at the harbor's entrance.

Everyone breathed an enormous sigh of relief at the enemy's departure. They'd survived and, even better, sunk a big enemy transport! Cloutier waited for the darkness to fall before resuming their course, and the Wahoo eventually surfaced to a lovely evening on the Pacific. The skipper opened the bridge's hatch and left the ship to take a breather; the air was rank in the submarine. Every sailor would get their five minutes of topside in the next hour. And then, the ship resumed its course toward Australia and its uncertain future since it just didn't have the supply and oil to get there.

The Japanese attack in the Coral Sea part 2

New Britain, Solomon Islands, and New Guinea, Apr-May 1942

The Japanese occupation of the Solomon Islands was another easy affair for the imperial forces. There were no Allied troops of any kind on the islands apart from listening stations and a couple of seaplane bases. They were quickly scattered on the Imperial Navy's approach.

The Jap forces landed important troops and equipment at Bougainville and Guadalcanal, intending to build major airbases to block any enemy shipping or naval vessel in the area. The intention was to have a chain of airfields with which to rebase the aircraft from Rabaul and thus have complete mastery of the air in the area.

It was a disaster from the Allied standpoint, but they couldn't do much against it. The Australians, as said previously, had already conceded everything that was not in their home country and could not have opposed the Imperial Navy in any significant way, even if they wanted to.

So, the affair was as simple as a logistical landing operation for the Japanese. By May 1st, work on the two airfields in Bougainville and Guadalcanal was underway.

The next order of business was the landings on the northern coast of New Guinea, again an easy operation since the Allies had conceded the area. The Japs first landed a battalion and then, on May 4th, an entire division. Work on airfields in Buna and Lae started in earnest. By May

7th, the whole region was under control; the Rabaul base was operational and sending regular airstrikes at Port Moresby. The Imperial Navy was considering sending its carrier force, which was unopposed since no Allied ships were in the area, raiding the Australian coast and harbor.

Furthermore, (another frightening aspect for the Australians), the Japanese 67th division that had landed at Lae started its trek through the Kokoda Track, the jungle road that crossed the New Guineans mountains to the southern coast and where Port Moresby lay. The Japanese Navy thus landed more supplies in preparation for the land attack there.

Things did not look good for Australia. The Japanese were cutting the sea lanes connecting it to North America, and Imperial forces approached the western parts of the country in its blazing conquest of the Dutch East Indies.

In fact, a disaster was in the making if the Allies didn't do anything about it.

U.S. leaders discuss the relief of Australia, May 9th, 1942

The writing was on the wall if nothing was done to correct the situation. Japan was utterly isolating Australia and New Zealand from the shipping lanes. Its forces were mopping up the Dutch East Indies, isolating the western part. The northern and eastern regions (Australia's access to the Pacific) were also slowly but surely occupied by the Imperial Navy, proof being the recent occupation of New Britain and the Solomon Islands. This was a horrible development for the overall Allied strategic situation. If Australia fell, then it would mean that Japan could re-direct its whole weight toward the Central Pacific and the USA. While there still was a good possibility that the proverbial industrial power of the land of the free would win in the end, it would cost so many more American lives and take so much time that President Roosevelt, General Marshall, and even stubborn Admiral King wanted to avoid it all cost. And there was also the fact that Australia was one of their best allies, and it was simply impossible to ignore their pleas for help. Japanese occupation and campaigning did not carry an excellent reputation.

The dreadful thing about it was that the Allies had no ships to oppose Japanese expansion in the south seas. In short, Admiral Yamamoto could do what he pleased, and the United States couldn't do much because of the fact that they'd lost Pearl Harbor and Samoa, so there was no refueling station or easy way to get to Oceania.

But then again, these were modern times, and sailing ships for an extended period was possible. It just wasn't efficient. U.S. ships could actually get to Australia via the open waters of the southern Pacific.

While possessing an abrasive and challenging personality, Admiral King was a brilliant man who'd found a solution to the U.S.-Australian predicament. He'd called a meeting with the president and the Commander In Chief General Marshall. Before doing so, he'd taken the time to meet with his best captains and admirals, who all concurred. The Navy could send a relief fleet to Australia. It would just take a long time, be complicated, and burn up a lot of fuel.

Using the route that King had in mind for the relief force was out of the question regarding regular shipping lanes, but it could be done for a one-of-a-kind operation. Oil tankers could also be laid along the fleet route so to replenish the ships that would need it, like the large battleships, but they had the range for a one-way trip anyway.

"So, Admiral King," started General Marshall. You have come up with a way to reinforce Australia with a fleet?" King put on his usual stern look and answered. "Yes, General. As you know, the normal sea lanes are being taken over by the Japs, and as such, most of the islands that could be used as refueling stations will be gone soon." The three men (the President was also there but remained silent, listening for the moment) in the room still had in mind the fresh losses of places like Samoa or Palmyra. "Yes, Admiral, we know, and that is why we have been intrigued by your meeting request," added Marshall, seemingly exasperated that King wasn't going to the heart of the matter at once. The stubborn Navy commander liked what he saw and loved to annoy the man, so he continued.

"The other problem was to find the ships without jeopardizing our coming attack on Hawaii or the ones we are planning against the Axis to retake the initiative and liberate the British Islands." He paused to fish out the large map in a box beside the table in the Oval Office, where the meeting was being held. "Ah, Admiral. We are finally getting to the main subject!" said a now enthusiastic Roosevelt. "Yes, Mr. President." He unrolled the map on the table between the two couches they were sitting on. "I present you the Milk Run," said King, pointing to a large arrow that circumvented the approximate extent of the Japanese realm in the Pacific or what they thought it would be soon. The other two men looking intently at the map, he continued. "The route is a less known sailing route and has been used by vessels since the age of sails. It isn't used as much nowadays, but we can still make it work. The fleet will first go through some Pacific Islands, with a major stop at Tahiti, a French territory. We can set up a refueling base there." Knowing what the following question from either Roosevelt or Marshall would be, he continued before they asked it. "The journey is 8000 nautical miles and will take around 20 days at 20 knots. Even the battleships can make it in a one-way trip if we want to." King finished, adding one of his rare smiles. The two other men, seemingly pleased, lifted up their eyes from the map. "Perfect, Admiral, seems you've got the route," said the President, who was now in an obviously happy mood. "So, now. Knowing you, what have you found to send there? We are already scraping the bottom of the barrel for all of our obligations around the world...."

"Mr. President, I did scrape it clean and found a decent fleet. We can spare the following from our forces: The two old aircraft carriers, Ranger and Charger, two equally old battleships (Utah and New York), two cruisers (the San Francisco and the Chicago), five aging light cruisers, and ten World War One destroyers that we have just reactivated." Marshall whistled softly, clearly impressed. But King wasn't done. "I've also contacted our British allies. They could also supply the old battleship Iron Duke and a cruiser, the London. Adding these units with the Australian Navy with two heavy cruisers, five destroyers, and three light cruisers, we would have ourselves a very decent fleet to oppose the damned Japs...."

It wasn't like the U.S. President would disapprove of this project. So the discussion continued for another ten minutes, after which King had his go-ahead to organize relief fleet Australia. The best-case scenario meant the ships would arrive sometime in June 1942, maybe even at the beginning of July. But it was better than not sending anything.

May 10-15th, 1942

After their landings and subsequent victory on the other Dutch Islands, including Java, the Japanese went for the kill and launched operations at the last two Dutch bastions in the Far East: The Islands of Ambon and Timor, both major military bases.

Ambon was the island which the colony got most of its native military recruits from. The people from those islands had been traditionally drafted into the Royal Dutch Forces for generations, supplanting most other populations across the colony. It, unfortunately, didn't mean that numerous troops defended it. Only a battalion of soldiers held the place. Like the rest of the Dutch campaign, the Japanese were vastly superior in soldiers, troops, and ships. No wonder, since the Nazis occupied the Netherlands in Europe, the country was far from being able to support a colony, let alone build up a military force to defend it.

Timor was the colony's major naval base. Not that it had any military ships to defend it when the time came for the enemy to invade the island. Dutch Naval power had been either sunk or put to flight earlier in the Japanese conquests. In practice, only a few submarines still survived.

By the time the Imperial Navy's transport, soldiers, and planes approached both islands, the defending force in Timor numbered just above 1500 men, while in Ambon (Ceram), it rose to 1700. Both the

Dutch (what was left of their forces), and the Australians sent troops to both islands to try and hold them.

They both faced well over their numbers. The IJA sent an entire division (the 52nd) to Timor while it sent one Marine Regiment in Ambon, supported by several special landing units (SLNF) battalions. With the given discrepancy in terms of airpower and Japanese naval supremacy, it wasn't like the struggle forecasted to be a contest.

The battle for Ambon was short and intense since Japanese superiority was so overwhelming that the fight lasted only two days. And so, the same pattern repeated itself, almost like a broken record: smashing airstrikes, earth-shattering shore bombardment, night landing, and then Japanese victory. On May 12th, it was all over, and all Allied forces in Ceram (Ambon) accepted surrender terms from the Japanese forces.

On Timor, things proved to be a little more complicated for Japan. First of all, the Japanese decided to land both in Dutch AND Portuguese Timor, not having a care in the world for a country's neutrality and not even bothering to declare war. The 52nd Division soon got into a fight reminiscent of the worst battles in China.

Australian and Dutch allies fought well, giving every inch of ground to the Japs in exchange for a heavy toll in casualties. After five days, the result was still inconclusive when the Australian Navy, with the Cruisers Canberra and Australia in the lead, forced the Japanese blockade and fought with an Imperial Navy task force composed of heavy cruisers Mogami and Mikuma.

The intense surface battle saw one of the first Allied successes of the war on the naval side. Both Australian ships, helped by their escorting light cruisers and destroyers, scored direct hits on the Nipponese vessels that retired in confusion, seriously damaged. The two Imperial cruisers got lucky that the Admiral in charge of the Aussie fleet had come to organize an evacuation of the Australo-Dutch force. The operation proceeded smoothly, albeit under fire from the guns of the Japanese 52nd Division. By the morning of the 16th of May, the Australian fleet was sailing back at full speed toward Darwin in Australia.

Admiral Raizo Ishaka, the head of the fleet responsible for the attack on Ceram and Timor, was enraged and sent his battleships to face the Australian Navy. Still, the Allies were gone by the time he got around Timor to bring his guns to bear.

So, the Japanese Army finished mopping up the rest of Timor's defenses and went into occupation mode. There would not be any more direct fights between armies in Timor. Still, the 52nd would be kept quite busy for the next few months with an intense guerilla war waged by the local population, helped by several Dutch and Australian soldiers left behind.

On the 17th, after assessing the major damage on Mogami and Mikuma, Admiral Ishaka ordered them sent back to Kure Shipyard in Japan for major repairs. The ship would be gone from the theater for a long time.

CHAPTER 5

Macarthur's departure

The commander makes his escape May 12th, 1942

As the situation continued to deteriorate for the Filipino American forces on the Bataan Peninsula, the rest of the Philippines was also steadily occupied island by island by the Japanese.

As the situation worsened everywhere and with the complete inability of the Allies to send any kind of relief force to the area or anywhere else in the Pacific for that matter, the U.S. president and the Australian leadership in Canberra started to see that Australia would be the last wall for the defense of democracy in the Pacific.

Australia felt cornered by the Japanese offensives in Timor and the Coral Sea and the bad news of Samoa's occupation by Imperial forces. They needed a war leader to organize the continent's defense.

Several cables from Australia to the President requested the famous General Macarthur's transfer, which was so gallantly resisting in Bataan without reinforcement, no air cover, no fleet, and no supplies. They wanted him in Australia for the new South Seas High Command headquarters taking shape after the destruction of ABDA command and the Dutch East Indies. In fact, they despaired for a natural war leader to come to their aid.

And President Roosevelt concurred. The Allies needed a strong commander for the brutal battle that Australia was about to face.

According to intelligence reports, the Japanese were already preparing to invade.

With Australia's leadership behind him to make a decision, he cabled Macarthur, who was cramped up in the Corregidor fortress. He ordered him to move to Australia. The great General, former Chief of Staff of the U.S. Army, and famous soldier was not initially interested in leaving his cherished Philippines. But Roosevelt insisted on several other cables, and most of his staff convinced him that he could have the means to come back and liberate the country by leaving the Philippines. But the man, in the end, was persuaded because he had his family with him. By leaving, he could bring them to Australia.

However, wishing to leave and actually escaping a besieged place in the middle of a war were two different things. A plan was quickly etched together that involved some daredevil tactics but had some chance to work. First, Macarthur would leave on a PT boat with a select number of people (officers from his staff and his family members); he would then ride at 40 knots toward Mindanao to an airfield still in Allied hands in the northern part of the island. The place was called the Del Monte Field, a large airfield used before the war by the Del Monte Company.

Under cover of darkness and in the early morning of the 12th, the PT Boat, with aboard Macarthur, his family, and some of his staff followers, sped out of the small Corregidor Fortress harbor to flee the Japanese naval blockade at Manilla Bay's entrance. By sheer luck, the high waves and low PT Boat silhouette were not spotted by the Japanese lookouts, usually quite sharp.

By daybreak, the weather deteriorated steadily, and towering waves buffeted the tiny, war-weary, blacked-out boat. The spray drove against their skin like stinging pellets of birdshot. The ship tossed crazily back and forth, seeming to hang free in space as though about to breach, and would then break away and go forward with a rush. The bad weather made for a rough ride, but it was a blessing for the hopeful escapee.

The boat rode in at full speed for most of the day and, by nightfall, was almost to Mindanao's northern coast, where the Del Monte airfield was located. Big foaming waves, fifteen or twenty feet high, thundered over the cockpit, drenching everybody. Their eyes were continuously drenched with stinging salt, so it was difficult for them to see, in addition to pitch-black visibility. But the PT Boat captain was an expert and had commanded such a vessel for years, so he did not waver.

Thus, they continued to speed through strange waters with islands all around them. They could also see the outlines of the big ones—Negros and Mindanao—very dimly against the horizon through the storm and the dark.

The following day, they finally reached the northern coast of Mindanao in broad daylight. It was a clear, dazzling day. Fortunately, no Japanese planes cut across the blue sky to attack or spot them.

By the time they finally hit land near the Del Monte field, two B-17s had been waiting for them. Another incredible feat for the Macarthur escape was that the two planes had flown – undetected - through Japanese-infested skies. They'd landed without a hitch, had been refueled, and were ready to fly again. It was about time that Macarthur and his entourage made it to the area, for the Japanese Army was advancing northward and was estimated to be about 20 miles from the airfield.

Not much time was wasted rushing everyone into one of the B-17s. The two bombers lifted off the long runway and took to the sky an hour after the PT Boat's arrival. They climbed to their maximum altitude of 35,000 feet, which enabled them to be relatively safe from Japanese planes. First, they could only be spotted with great difficulty, and second, their great speed for a bomber would allow them to speed away from any aircraft trying to intercept them. A zero fighter could go to 38 00 feet, but at those altitudes, fighters tended to lose much of their agility because of the thin air and were easier targets for the Flying Fortress' gunners.

In any case, the flight was uneventful, and the General landed in Darwin after a journey of thousands of miles.

The siege and the final fall, May 15th-21st 1942

A simple fact remained in the battle for the Bataan Peninsula and the Corregidor fortress. The Japanese did not break through because the US and Filipino forces faltered. They simply lost to exhaustion, lack of supplies, and total isolation from the rest of the Allied countries. From the time the campaign started to its end on May 22nd, 1942, not one pound of supplies or food was sent to the Bataan Peninsula.

It wasn't for lack of wanting, but it was more because events elsewhere in the Pacific blocked the Allies from sending any sort of

relief mission. While he was still in command of the Philippines forces, Macarthur clamored for reinforcements, for something to be done to help his beleaguered troops. But it was to no avail.

Things deteriorated considerably after the famous general was ordered back to Australia by the U.S. President. Not because of his absence but simply because the American-Filipino forces had merely reached the end of their incredible and heroic resistance. Most had been on quarter rations for weeks, and the ammunition levels had dropped to critical by the 19th of May while the fighting was heaviest.

In the weeks and months of battle, the Allied forces fought a brilliant fighting retreat downward in the Peninsula, with good defenses and well-prepared positions. The Japanese despaired for a long while because they simply couldn't advance. For them, it was an ominous sign of things to come; under the right conditions, the U.S. Army and Marines were better trained and equipped than most Japanese counterparts. Maybe the going would have been easier for the Nipponese if they'd had their Imperial Guards Division or 18th Division in the Philippines, but such as the situation was, they didn't. And one fact remained. The average Japanese division was not up to face a modern army with tanks and all the modern weaponry the Americans brought to battle from 1943 onward.

Needing to finish the job and destroy the American Army once and for all, and after many failed attacks and high casualties, the Imperial Army HQ (General Hajime) sent strong artillery forces to the Philippines to smash the American fortifications.

The Imperial Army thus landed over two hundred heavy artillery guns north of the American Bataan Peninsula, like the 150 mm cannons and the rare Type 45 240 mm howitzer. Japanese General Homma's 14th Imperial Army was also heavily reinforced by an additional three divisions, and toward the middle of May, the Japanese forces prepared for the final assault.

On May 15th, the Allied defenses were smashed with a ton of shells and bombs for the entire day, which turned the weakened American defenses into an inferno. For the next three days, the Nipponese forces pushed the Americano-Filipino forces back southward.

The fight lasted a lot shorter than what Homma had expected, thinking that the last push should have taken him a week to two weeks to reduce the last bits of Allied resistance in the area. But the Allies were simply out of ammo and energy and without their inspiring commander.

All along the battlefront, units of the 1st U.S. Corps and the depleted remnants of the 2nd U.S. Corps crumbled in place. The defense thus shattered into small groups and knots of resistance. The American high command lost cohesion and communication with most of its frontline units. For the next four days, the entire Allied defensive perimeter progressively disintegrated and collapsed. By May 23rd, it was all over, and MacArthur's replacement in Bataan, Major General Edward P. King, surrendered his forces.

The strategic context, end of May 1942

After the fall of Singapore, the conquest of Pearl Harbor, and the Pacific Islands that blocked the sea lanes, the Australian government and many of its constituents feared Japan would invade the mainland. The recent fall of the Dutch East Indies did nothing to lessen those fears, as Japanese forces were now within range of the country's west coast. It also looked like the Fijis and the New Hebrides would soon fall as there were strong indications that the Imperial Navy was to move against them. Finally, the Japanese landings on the northern coast of New Guinea indicated that Port Moresby would soon be attacked and, in all likelihood, conquered. The country didn't have much to oppose the Japanese with. A battle loomed in the rough mountains between the Jap bases in the north and Port Moresby. A battle that Australia did not think it could win.

The country would be completely isolated from the other Allies, and the Japanese could attack at will. The problem was compounded by the fact that the Australian land army was not ready to repulse an enemy assault. The 8th Division, scattered around the Dutch East Indies and Malaya, was gone, with its soldiers either killed or captive. Three more units were in Africa, and while they'd been recalled (5th, 6th, and 7th), it would take time to disengage them from the Agadir frontline and a challenge to get them through the Imperial Navy ships that were sure to try and sink them. The Militia was mobilized, but although a large force, it was inexperienced and lacked modern equipment. And so, in terms of land forces, the country was defended by four divisions in total (1st to 4th). The areas that the RAA (Royal Australian Army) had to defend were so large and so widespread that it wasn't even a discussion to try to block the enemy from landing. The only thing that could be contemplated was the major cities and harbor defenses, like Darwin, Melbourne, Brisbane, and the like.

The Royal Australian Air Force (RAAF) lacked modern aircraft, and the Royal Australian Navy (RAN) was too small to counter the Imperial Japanese Navy.

In response to the threat, the government (Prime Minister John Curtin) appealed to the United States for assistance. Roosevelt responded by getting Macarthur out of the doomed Philippines theater and promising to send a relief fleet (already en route) through the Pacific's open waters to circumvent Japanese supremacy of the normal shipping lanes. The relief fleet also included land forces, Marines, artillery, planes, and others that would be handy when the Japanese onslaught came.

On the other side of the chessboard, the Japanese Army had decided to invade Australia, against Yamamoto's warning that Japan was truly over-extending itself with such an enormous undertaking as conquering a continent. Yamamoto judged the adventure to be beyond Japanese capabilities. But the Army, with Prime Minister Tojo and General Hajime in the lead, decided they could do it. The IJA came out of a very successful campaign in Southeast Asia and believed that nothing could stop the Nipponese tide. And until further notice, it remained to be proven that the Allies could oppose them in any serious way.

So by May 1942, the Grand Admiral decided to make the best of a bad situation and continued on his strategy of isolating Australia from the United States and preventing Allied offensive operations with the execution of the following operations: The capture of Port Moresby, consolidation of the Navy's presence in the Solomon Islands, the conquest of the Fiji, consolidation in Samoa and occupation of New Caledonia. With these feats achieved, at least Yamamoto thought he gave a chance to the Army's folly of capturing Oceania. While he knew he could take all those islands and areas, he didn't know if Japan could build up the necessary forces (planes, airfields, ships) to use them properly against the Allies.

It would all come down to what the Allies would decide to do. They currently were in a defensive stance that advocated passivity in front of the Japanese strategic initiative.

Yamamoto didn't know it yet, but the Allied strategy was about to take a new direction under the guidance of a new, energetic General, Douglas Macarthur. A fleet was also coming to shore up the naval forces, which would prove decisive in the battles of the next few months.

The battle for Port Moresby part 1
May 17th-28th 1942

As mentioned, the Japanese landed the 67th division in Lae (northern New Guinea). It didn't take long for these forces to mop up the feeble defense in the area. And then they started their trek thru the Kokoda Track, the jungle road that crossed the New Guinean mountains to the southern coast and where Port Moresby lay. The Japanese Navy also continued to land more supplies in preparation for the offensive.

On the other side of the mountains, the Australians awaited the Japs with only a battalion of men. Some preparations were taken in the city, but it was decided to move the unit into the Kokoda track and fight the enemy where the terrain was most suited for defense.

In 1942, Papua was an Australian territory. There had been little development in the area, and it was largely devoid of infrastructure beyond that around Port Moresby. The administrative center had basic airfield and port facilities. It was nothing impressive in civilian terms, but for both sides in the war, it meant a potential base that could be expanded. Also, for Australia, it was considered its northern shield; as long as it held, the enemy was further away from the country. For Japan and men like the Grand Admiral, it was the prerequisite for more attacks on Australia's northern coast.

The area around Port Moresby had no modern roads and everything was done through native tracks. Most of the traveling in and around Papua was done by air or sea. The Japanese would have been better served by landing directly on the southern side. Still, their transport capability was somewhat limited, as it was busy transporting troops for operations all across the Pacific theater.

The Kokoda Track was a trail that ran across the Owen Stanley Range. From the Japanese perspective, it looked doable to take the track with their troops and cross the mountain range to get to the other side. It certainly looked like the shortest route. They learned of its existence through trough vague explorer's accounts; it offered a quick solution to how to get to Port Moresby. Besides, their amphibious and transport assets were busy conquering the Dutch East Indies, Southeast Asia, and the like; thus, it was their only viable option in the short term.

The track climbed to 7200 feet as it ran through the jagged peaks and disease-infested jungle of the Owen Stanley Range. This was not going to be a cakewalk for the Japanese.

The Imperial troops climbed high and mighty in the trail. Still, after two days of struggle with the weather, the flies, and the rugged terrain, the decision was taken to abandon the tanks (only for the time being). Some Type 95s had been landed with the forces in Lae and Buna but were turned back because the terrain was unsuitable for anything motorized.

On the 20th, the Japanese forward element came in contact with the Australian defenses near Mount Bellamy. The Aussies had done a great job of preparing decent positions and stopped the 67th first and second battalions dead in their tracks. The battle raged for a day, after which the Imperial forces decided to retire a kilometer backward in confusion. The Japanese commander (General Harukichi Hyakutake) raged and sent more force in direct frontal assaults but to no avail. The Allied soldiers were positioned in a narrow part of the track, surrounded by towering rock faces. So, even their small force could hold infinite enemies because they didn't have any heavy artillery or guns. The Australians had found their Thermopylae.

The Japanese invasion of the Fijis and New Hebrides

The Imperial Navy seize Noumea and the rest, May 11-17th, 1942

After the imperial offensives of March and April, the Fijis to the southeast of the Solomons, New Caledonia, and the New Hebrides (Vanuatu) found themselves on the front line of the Pacific War.

Three different countries/colonies/sets of Islands, but with one similarity: The Japanese Grand Admiral had included them in his strategic planning for the war in the Pacific.

FIJIS: Suva in Fiji boasted one of the finest natural harbors in the South Pacific - three miles wide and cutting two miles inland. It also had one of the only paved airfields in the area. The Imperial Navy planned to make it into a great airbase. It wasn't the colony with the most resources, but its main attraction for the Japanese was its position in the Pacific, where it could block Allied shipping lanes to Australia.

NEW HEBRIDES: The New Hebrides was a Franco-British colony boasting over eighty islands. Its infrastructures were non-existent in 1942, but they offered a great strategic position as part of the Japanese plan of occupying New Caledonia and the Fijis. The Japanese had several plans in place to build airfields. Whether they would have time or resources to do so was still in question (The Japanese were building airfields and harbor bases all over the Pacific at this time). But the worst-case scenario for Yamamoto was that at least it would be garrisoned with Japanese troops.

NEW CALEDONIA: The large island not only had rich nickel deposits, which the Japanese Empire needed, but it also possessed a somewhat modern harbor and was strategically situated between Samoa and Australia. It was the Allied convoy route's waypoint toward Australia. Its capture would greatly hamper any U.S. effort to supply and relieve Australia. It was a French territory and thus not well defended since De Gaulle and Petain, quite busy with their European affairs against the Germans, had not bothered to send reinforcement or properly supply the troops already in place.

On May 12, a small Imperial Navy task force arrived in the New Hebrides with over 1100 men. The force was composed only of seven destroyers and two large transports. It was unprepared to face any enemy fleet, but none had been reported in the area. And so it went about dropping detachments on every island that mattered. By the 15th, it was all over, and all the soldiers had been landed. Six of the destroyers and the transports left for Truk, while one ship (a destroyer) stayed in Port Vila as a patrol ship. Several seaplanes were also dropped from the transport to organize an efficient air patrol game plan.

The story was much the same in Fiji, with not much in the way of defense on Suva. The small militia detachment was quickly scattered by the destroyers that arrived in the harbor. The imperial fleet came at the Fijis with two light cruisers, four destroyers, and two small troop transports. They landed just over 800 men on the islands, especially on Suva, where the airport and deep-water port were located. It was all over by the 13th of May, and the Japanese flag floated over the British colony.

The going was a little more "difficult" in New Caledonia, where the Free French had a garrison. It wasn't the best equipped or the most numerous and was essentially composed of militia, but it was still something to defend the island with. The Japanese made their run at the place with the full weight of their main Coral Sea task force. Indeed, Yamamoto had sent some reinforcements to the area from Pearl Harbor, given the relative American inactivity after their major Pearl Harbor defeat. Fleet carriers Soryu and Hiryu, along with battleships Haruna/Kongo, heavy cruiser Suzuya, and four destroyers. And the pattern of conquest so far executed by the Japanese Navy was again rehearsed. Carrier strikes on the main military facilities and troops, shore-bombardment operations by the big guns, landing at night by the elite Marine battalion. By midday on the 14th, it was already over. The French governor surrendered New Caledonia.

In one last bold stroke, Yamamoto had closed the ring around Australia. Japan was now poised to make its killing.

A new command, May 28th, 1942

I arrived by train in Melbourne after my harrowing escape from the Philippines and a very long B-17 flight from the Del Monte Airfield on Mindanao to Australia's West Coast (Darwin) and then by train to the Australian capital. Australia's situation was as dark as the Philippines' before being invaded. Encircled on every side, isolated, and outnumbered, it didn't look like it would be able to stop the Japanese tide blanketing the Pacific. The Allies needed a strategy and some strong morale-boosting, for it was on the verge of being invaded. On my train ride, I was able to read several of the newspapers (the recent ones and several outdated ones), and I understood the definite sense of defeatism engulfing the Aussies.

Prime Minister John Curtin, the very man responsible for my arrival in Australia (he had petitioned President Roosevelt to order me out of the Philippines to take command of the Southwest Allied forces), was waiting for me at the dock, and we shook hands, our professional relationship taking off right away. From the very start, we both got a real sense of cooperation and friendship. We immediately went into a meeting, where food and drinks were served, and we discussed at length what were the next steps in the war. We both agreed that our countries were intricately linked to the final victory and that, as such, we would fight the difficult battles ahead as true friends and allies. Without the United States, Australia was doomed to be occupied as it did not have the industrial infrastructure to produce the means of war needed to fight the Japanese juggernaut. In an equal measure, the U.S. needed Australia as a steppingstone and as a way to fight the Japs. With no more islands to call home in the Pacific, the loss of Australia would have meant the end of the Pacific War because it would not have been possible to bring the war to the enemy.

The immediate and imperative challenge to tackle was Australia's defense with what we had, which wasn't much. The military situation was abysmal. The Australian military was weak, with a part of its force fighting abroad in Africa, and it faced an imminent Japanese invasion, especially on the West Coast (Darwin) and New Guinea.

A third of its ground troops were in the Middle East, while the United States had only one division present and only partially trained. Its air force was equipped with almost obsolete planes and lacked engines, spare parts, and personnel. Its navy had no carriers or battleships.

Also, it was completely, utterly isolated. With the seizure by the Japanese of the New Hebrides and New Caledonia, and finally, the Fiji Islands, all shipping sea lanes were closed to the country. In the west, it was also blocked since there were as many Japanese bayonets as possible and ships with the recent conquest of the Dutch East Indies by Japan.

The outlook was bleak.

Having seen the enemy blitzkrieg of Hong Kong, Thailand, Malaya, Rabat, the Dutch Colony, the Solomons, New Britain, and all the other islands (not to forget the terrible American defeat in the Philippines and Pearl Harbor), the Australians could only thing defensively. But the main thing here was to try and wrestle the initiative out of Japanese hands in any way we could

As it was, the Australians were already defending the Kokoda Track against odds ten times their numbers, so why the hell was it not possible to defeat the damned Japs if we sent more troops? Upon my arrival in full command after the meeting with the Prime Minister, I ordered the immediate reinforcement of the Port Moresby base with the shipping of the 1st Division. The Royal Australian Navy and its first fleet, so recently successful in Timor with a naval victory, was tasked with escorting the troops. As I knew there was a strong naval Imperial Navy presence in the Coral Sea, I also ordered the immediate transfer of all available air assets to the small airfields on the northern coast and in New Guinea proper. The planes were mostly outdated Brewster Buffalos and other types like that, but we did have a good fifty sturdy P-40 Warhawk in our arsenal. By bunching up everything we had, I believed we could successfully run the Japanese gauntlet and get reinforcements and supplies through.

If successful, this would save Australia from invasion (at least from the north side and where it was important to hold) and allow me to pass from defense to offense, seize the initiative, move forward, and attack.

This decision gave the Australians an exhilarating lift, and they prepared to support me with almost fanatical zeal. As a matter of fact, throughout the war, the most complete cooperation existed with the Australians and the other nationalities under my command—Dutch, British, New Zealanders, and Filipinos. Not only

was there a complete lack of friction and misunderstanding, but the ties of mutual respect, goodwill, and admiration among the commanders, staff, and men of all branches and services could well serve as a model for any mixed international force. The full confidence of these nations and their forces, of such marked native variance, was an important factor in the success of the Pacific war.

The Aussies needed to put some spine into their resolve, and we did just that with the Port Moresby campaign and the stand we took against Japanese aggression.

Carrier landing

Bergman training as a carrier pilot, May 29th, 1942

"Easy, now," said Harry to himself. He was again sitting in the cockpit of an SBD Dauntless dive bomber, approaching the fleet aircraft carrier Hornet. He was rehearsing his instructor's words. "Remember, now. The length of the landing strip is quite short on a carrier, so you need to approach at a slower speed than a normal airplane. You can also use the wind if you are facing it, as it can compensate for the speed instead of putting down your flaps."

He was flying against a strong wind, so he used it to better his landing. He moved his flight stick toward him a little for the plane to catch more of the wind. "Yes, that did the trick," he muttered again. And then the carrier deck was just above him, and he touched down with the aircraft's wheels.

The Dauntless sped up on the steel runway, and he pushed on the brakes as hard as he could. The end of the Hornet was nearing, and he could already see the blue sea behind it when the hook under his plane caught one of the final stopping cables, jerking his aircraft back, stopping it cold.

He'd again done it. His. After five successful landings, he was finally considered to be fit for carrier duty. The signalman on the deck approached his plane and gestured for him to roll the plane to the side. More SBDs were about to land behind Bergman.

He did as heinstructed, parked his plane by the large carrier elevator (the plane would go down in the ship's belly to be stored and for maintenance), and walked the distance to the conning tower to enter the bowels of the vessel.

After his stint with the attack on the Japanese fleet, Harry had flown back to base and had thought nothing more of it than a soldier doing

his duty, but his superiors had been impressed. They'd told him he'd shown great promise as a dive bomber pilot. His ability to follow the lead and even execute an attack on a Japanese ship was apparently very difficult, earmarking him as a natural for the job.

And so he'd rapidly been ordered to a training base for carrier pilots, where they'd received a crash course in landing and taking off. The training was nothing more than taking off and landing on a smaller airfield the length of a carrier. They'd also been followed by several carrier pilots transferred for the training of hundreds of other men like Harry.

America was gearing up for war, so men from across the country flocked to western airfield training bases to become Navy pilots. There were talks of dozens upon dozens of carriers being laid down in the shipyards, and for that, the fleet would need pilots to man the planes that would be included with those flattops.

Harry's last landing meant he was considered fit for full duty on the Hornet and had already been told as much. The ship was cruising lazily off the Mexican waters, far away from any potential Japanese attacks. Its regular pilots had gone to San Diego to defend the base and launch a strike at the Imperial Navy if it chose to show itself back there. The carrier took in the best and most promising of the new SBD Dauntless recruits and had been busy training them for the last week.

Bergman was happy as he walked to the officer's mess for a hot meal and some downtime. Soon, the carrier would get its first war mission, and Harry would have to fight another battle.

The RAN braves the Japanese naval gauntlet May 31st, 1942

On the same day he took command (May 28th) and following the news of the Australian success in the Kokoda Track, General Macarthur gave the order for the whole of the RAN (Royal Australian Navy) to assemble in Cairns in anticipation of the transport of a full division to Port Moresby.

The American General, now the new overall commander of the Southwest Pacific Area Command (SWPA), instilled a jolt of energy in the beleaguered and frightened Australians. The Allies were done with passive defense. And so, Macarthur had again exercised his incredible energy and initiative. In his own words: "It is about time we do something else than defending against the Japs."

Port Moresby needed to be held at all costs; to do that, the Australians would send everything they had at it. After all, if the town stayed in Allied hands, Japan would not invade the northern coast of Australia. The entire first division would thus be sent to New Guinea, along with the only heavy artillery regiment the Allies had available in the theater. Along for the ride would also be a battalion of Marines. "The General" (as the troops affectionately called Macarthur) firmly believed that the Allies would hold the line against the Japanese onslaught.

The fleet gathered by the Australian Navy was pretty much the same that had mauled the two Japanese vessels a few weeks back. It was led by two heavy cruisers, the Canberra and the Australia. Five destroyers were also along for the ride and three light cruisers. In terms of air coverage, Macarthur had assembled everything available. From the forty surviving Dutch planes (Brewster Buffalo's), fifty Warhawk, and about another eighty or so hodgepodge of aircraft that could be called fighters from the Australian Army. Their job was to cover the fleet against any Japanese air attacks. Also included in the task force was the seaplane tender Albatross. It would not be much of a help against top-of-the-line Zero fighters, but it was what the Allies had, so that was that. In the center of the task force were thirty-two transports of all shapes and sizes, carrying the troops before-mentioned.

The fleet left the vicinity of Cairns harbor in all haste on the 31st. Not everything was perfect and ready, but speed was of the essence for Macarthur, so he removed all the "red tape" administrative aspects of the troop transport and gathering, leaving the operation's command to Vice-Admiral Sir John Augustine Collins. It was a chaotic affair, but the task force – and its vital cargo – left on schedule.

A Japanese response was expected, and it didn't take long to become a reality. In the first few hours of the voyage, a large Japanese fleet was spotted east of the RAN fleet. It was the very same one that had just completed the conquest of New Caledonia and the other islands: Fleet carriers Hiryu, Soryu, light carriers Zhuiho, Ryujo (total of 150 planes) battleships Haruna and Kongo heavy cruisers Suzuya, with new arrivals Atago and Haguro. Eight light cruisers and twelve destroyers escorted them. It was a mighty task force given the mission of enforcing a full blockade of Australia's northern coast, Port Moresby, and the Coral Sea.

It was also determined that the Japanese had sent a strike against the transport fleet from the moment it was spotted. Everything available on the Allied side scrambled over Collin's ships. An hour into the planes moving toward each other, they met above the Allied fleet. The Allies had gathered 160 aircraft, while the Japanese had 150.

The ensuing dogfight battle was an epic affair of desperation on the Allied side and of killing on the Japanese side. All the while, the Australo-Americans also launched a fleet of dive (there were about twenty-five SBD Dauntless in Macarthur's command) from Cairns.

Of course, the air battle ended in a Japanese victory; the Nipponese pilots got over sixty victories in the sky, while the Allies enacted a little over twenty kills on their side. And then the Imperial Navy pilot plunged toward the RAN fleet. The Australians fired with everything they had at their enemies, filling the sky with red tracer flak ordinance lines. Several Japanese planes were again destroyed, crashing in flames in the water. And then the thirty or so torpedo bombers made their run at the Allied fleet, launching their weapons from short range. The whole fleet tried to dodge in frantic maneuvers, but the destroyers did their dreadful job. They put themselves between the ships and the torpedoes, taking hits that would have been on transport ships instead. The five RAN destroyers were thus obliterated. Canberra was also hit with a torpedo but continued on its course while taking in water. Four transports were also sunk, taking with them over 1800 souls and much military equipment to the bottom. And then the Japanese air armada left the vicinity. Admiral Collins ordered the fleet to continue at full speed toward Port Moresby. They, unfortunately, had to leave their stricken sailors in the sea to their own devices. Time was of the essence, and it was figured that the Japs would be back with another strike.

By the time the Jap aircraft turned around to return to their carriers, the SBD Dauntless planes from Cairns had arrived over the Imperial fleet. They were met by the CAP (combat air patrol), and eight of them got shot down outright, while the Japanese flak downed another six.

The eleven leftovers dove toward the battleship Haruna and carrier Hiryu. And they were rewarded with some decent hits. The Haruna got a bomb right on its deck. It plunged into the ship's bowels and exploded, creating a powerful fire and seriously wounding the ship. Hiryu received a bomb right on its flight deck. The resulting explosion made a big hole, rendering all air operations impossible for that day. Most of the planes were either redirected to Hiryu or the other light carriers, crowding the Japanese decks and making it

impossible to organize another strike during the battle.

The Japanese admiral in charge of the 2nd fleet, Admiral Shigeyoshi Inoue, decided, looking at his flaming and burning capital ships, that

he'd done enough for the day.

He had no way of knowing that the Allies had expanded everything they had and that they would not be able to do much more. But like every Japanese Admiral in the Imperial Navy, he had his standing orders; "conserve resources and DO NOT lose capital ships." He ordered his task force back to Rabaul for repairs. The Haruna and Hiryu would have to sail to the Truk base where the fleet repair ship was anchored, and the necessary facilities resided.

Some seven hours later, the Australian fleet arrived in Port Moresby, welcomed as saviors. The ships unloaded their cargoes and had to endure several Japanese airstrikes, but in the end, the town's air defenses, and the ship's flak guns protected most. Another hit was scored on a light cruiser, and a bomb landed on Australia's forward turret (seriously damaging it). The port facilities were wrecked, and hundreds of civilians died in the enemy raids. But by the 1st of June, the division and Marines were on the ground in Port Moresby.

Macarthur's gamble had paid off, and the Allies were finally striking back. The whole affair was an incredible boost to the beleaguered Australians.

Amatsukaze during the first battle of the Coral Sea, May 31st, 1942

After the action at Christmas Island, Amatsukaze was ordered to Rabaul in New Britain for new offensive operations in the Coral Sea. My ship arrived too late to participate in the triple invasions of the Hebrides, Caledonia, and Fijis, but we still rejoined the fleet as it was sailing back through the Solomon Islands.

Then, quite suddenly, our new commander, Admiral Shio, ordered the fleet south and west. Some Allied movements were reported, and Imperial Command also gave us the task of ensuring that no ships would either leave or enter Australia's northern and eastern coasts.

The goal was a total blockade of the continent to starve the Australians into surrendering. Without American help, it was thought that they would be unable to hold out.

By midday on the 31st, we were cruising about four hundred miles from the New Guinean Coast, as our orders were to intercept ships either going through the area between Cairns and Port Moresby (heavy traffic was reported by air recon) or else launch an airstrike on the city.

A general alarm sounded across the fleet as Admiral Shio received words that our seaplanes had spotted a sizeable Allied task force heading full-ahead toward Port Moresby. It didn't take more for the fleet's planes, from the great Soryu and Hiryu and the two light carriers Ryujo and

Zhuiho, to scramble and fly their aircraft to the western horizon to intercept.

A gathering airstrike is a sight to behold. The planes lifted off the carriers one after the other, then circled the fleet. They waited for the rest of their comrades to fly up and went away in a coordinated fashion toward the objective.

Our task force was quite powerful, boasting the above-mentioned flattops, along with three heavy cruisers and two mighty battleships. We'd left Ishaka's fleet for another strong one!

A couple of hours went by while we awaited the return of our planes and anxiously anticipated the results. We were confident. Didn't we conquer all of Southeast Asia and destroy everything in our paths? As we were daydreaming about more victories, another general alarm sounded. This time, it was warning us of an impending air raid.

We saw the Zero fighters thunder above us with a great noise as they pushed their engines to the maximum. The pilots headed toward the southern horizon, where we eventually saw several black dots approaching our vessels.

The numbers of fighters above our fleet were minimal, and I thus ordered every gunner to their battle stations as I expected some Allied planes to break through. Our job as a destroyer was to shoot down the enemy and protect the capital ships.

In the distance, we witnessed the dogfight, with planes going and zipping by. Tracers and some explosions were even seen as our brave flyers shot down some enemy bombers. Eventually, some of the American black dots got bigger and bigger until we could distinguish that they were SBD Dauntless planes with the U.S. star under their wing. They came at us from high up, and we fired with everything we had. The whole fleet did, creating one impressive firework that ended up blanketing the sky with dark explosions.

I remember being quite impressed at the number of tracer shells we shot together as a group of ships. Ultimately, about ten of the Dauntless got through and plunged toward our gunnery screen. Two of them scored hits on first Haruna and then Hiryu. For our part, we were narrowly missed by a bomb. It exploded not ten meters from Amatsukaze and lifted an enormous geyser of water that drenched us all on the decks. And then, the raid was over.

Twenty minutes later, our own planes came back from their airstrike at the enemy fleet. The reports were good; they'd scored several hits and sunk over seven ships.

I remember that my crew and I felt delighted at the prospect of continuing the destruction of the Australian fleet. Still, Admiral Oshio ordered a complete turnaround of the task force, and we were to head back to Rabaul.

It turned out that the hits on our two capital ships removed all the courage from our Admiral. The orders to "conserve resources at all costs" and losing a battleship or a carrier were tantamount to a major disaster; our commander didn't take a chance. After all, the Allies could always have sent more planes.

Only after the war did we learn that we'd cleaned the whole slate of Allied planes and that we could have sunk the relief fleet with our powerful surface units. It would have saved many Japanese lives and changed the Australian campaign's outcome. Port Moresby would undoubtedly have fallen.

But at the same time, we must praise General Macarthur, who was bold enough to show us that we were not as invincible as we thought we'd become.

The Australian relief fleet

Leahy arrives in Auckland, June 2nd, 1942

Admiral William D. Leahy, commander of the Australia relief fleet, more formally known as the 6th U.S. fleet, stood on the battleship Utah Bridge, looking out through the viewport toward the New Zealand coast.

As Chief of Naval Operations from 1937 to 1939, he was the senior officer in the United States Navy, overseeing the preparations for war. After retiring from the Navy, he was appointed in 1939 by his close friend, President Franklin D. Roosevelt, as the governor of Puerto Rico.

But then the war happened. At first, he stayed on the sidelines, but like General Douglas Macarthur, he was a man of action and couldn't stay in retirement. So, he soon lobbied for a new position within the U.S. Navy. The President already had his fighting admirals in key places, but then the Australian relief fleet opportunity presented itself, and Roosevelt rapidly called his friend. The President also offered him the position of his personal chief of staff, but the Admiral preferred to be in the thick of the action. And so, he took on the challenge of a command to save Australia. He would have to work with Douglas Macarthur, an old acquaintance for the men who had been chief of staff of the U.S. Army, so they'd known each other well.

Another reason he wanted the command was that, as a Midshipman, Leahy had been assigned to the USS Oregon. He was on that battleship when she made her famous dash through the Strait of Magellan and around South America in the spring of 1898 to participate in the Battle of Santiago on July 3 during the Spanish American War. He was pretty angry at the ship's destruction during the early days of the war and wanted to get back at the Japanese for destroying it and killing many people he knew on that vessel.

The 6th fleet was a scratch force of many ships, and at the same time, it was quite powerful. Centered around the fleet carrier Ranger and the light carrier Charger, it also sported four battleships. Three of them were American (Utah, New York, and Washington), and the fourth was British (Iron Duke). The fleet had the London (again supplied by the Royal Navy), the San Francisco, and the Chicago in terms of cruisers. The escort ships were not numerous but would have to do: five light cruisers and twelve World War One destroyers that had just been reactivated from the East Coast mothball fleet.

It wasn't the most powerful force the Americans could send, but then again, they had other theaters of operation. First and foremost, things were brewing in Europe, and they needed a lot of ships to keep the mastery of the Atlantic. They also needed them for their eventual reconquest of the United Kingdom and as escort/support for their North African campaign. And then the rest of the Navy's hitting power concentrated in San Diego for the expected offensive against Oahu. Without Pearl Harbor, no serious U.S. campaign could have been conducted to liberate the Pacific.

Yes, the Allies could send the 6th fleet to Australia's help as a stop-gap measure, but the whole affair could not be organized from something so far away and challenging to get to.

The voyage through the "milk run," as it was called, the approximate sea lane going through the open Pacific and then to Tahiti to New Zealand, had been somewhat uneventful. They sailed around the extreme range of the Japanese realm. The Imperial Navy was powerful, but it wasn't omnipotent. It was still in the process of occupying and consolidating its new possessions in the Pacific, so it was beyond its capabilities to intercept a fleet that sailed so far from its main base. Hence the reason the Americans had sent the fleet in that direction.

If the 6th fleet was powerful, it would be an opposing force even more powerful. According to the latest intelligence estimates, the

Japs had two fleets within Australia's vicinity. The 2nd fleet, the one that had just fought against the Royal Australian Navy near Port Moresby, was already as strong as Leahy's task force with two battleships, two fleet carriers, two light carriers, at least three heavy cruisers, from five to ten light cruisers and over fifteen destroyers.

Then, another fleet roamed the waves east of Timor and was currently raiding the Australian coast. That fleet had one light carrier, four battleships, four heavy cruisers, over ten light cruisers, and at least twenty destroyers.

While some of those ships were expected back in Pearl Harbor at some point because Yamamoto was sure to concentrate his force there to fight the sizeable American force gathering in San Diego, in the meantime, it represented a significant problem for Macarthur and his SWPA command.

As he got ready to go ashore in Auckland, New Zealand (his motorboat was ready), Leahy wondered what battles lay ahead.

One thing was sure. It was going to be a tight one. But at least now Australia had a fleet to defend it.

Kokoda positions and counter-attack June 3-4th, 1942

The Kokoda Track was not a nice place to have a stroll. On the contrary, it was anything but. It also was not a place to have a fight in. The track threaded 96 kilometers across the Owen Stanley Range — harsh, jagged peaks clad in dense rain-soaked tropical jungle.

A lone, well-equipped man would take at least ten days to get through it—an army, weeks. The paths were steep, narrow, slippery, and a perfect ambush zone. Soldiers in coastal areas like Port Moresby or the northern beachheads of Guna and Buna were also fighting in the world's most malarial, mosquito-ridden area.

Since the start of the campaign almost three weeks before, sickness had so far claimed more men than combat (approximately 325 Australians and 1200 Japanese). Any injury or bleeding could mean an infection, and that was when a soldier wasn't bitten by a malaria-infected mosquito. The whole affair was on foot only, with artillery brought to the front with great difficulty, tanks or anything motorized beyond any possibility. It rained every day, and the humidity was unbearable. The constant water downpour transformed the track into mud tangles, and it was a terrible sight to behold.

The two armies fought each other high in the mountain range near Mount Bellamy, and the Aussie battalion fought odds ten times its numbers. They'd found a position where they blocked the track between towering rockfaces, so the Japanese forces floundered before them. Casualties were terrible on the IJA's side, and they eventually retreated to regroup.

The time they took for regrouping was used by the newly landed (and fresh) Australian 1st Division and their U.S. Marines allies to move up the Owen Stanley's through the Kokoda track. The unit's men went directly to the battlefield from the boats in Port Moresby's harbor.

They arrived just in time for a renewed Japanese assault. The Nipponese had been able to bring (with great difficulty) two 140mm Howitzers from the coast and opened up with them and blasted the thin Australian defense line between the rocks. As General Harukichi Hyakutake, the Japanese force commander, sent his men forward in great shouts of "Banzai!" the brave men that had been defending against all odds retreated in haste.

And thus, for a moment, the imperial soldiers thought they'd won and would be able to march into Port Moresby and claim victory. But the men of the new units arrived, rallied the fleeing troops that took heart at the sight of their fresh comrades, and hastily organized a counterattack.

What followed next was a confused battle that lasted for two days, where attacks and counterattacks succeeded each other. The narrowness of the track meant that it was simply impossible to win the day in a landslide battle, rout, or outflanking. Whenever a group of men would get broken or killed, thus creating an opening, there would always be a layer of new men at the ready further down the track to stop any decisive breakthrough.

On the 4th of June, General Hyakutake was the first to recognize that his attempts were futile. He might have had a chance before the Allied reinforcements, but with the added strength of the new units, he deemed the whole thing improbable.

He ordered the 67th Division (or what was left of it) to retire several kilometers behind the frontline and set in pre-prepared defensive positions. He also chose a spot with wide enough ground so he could use more men for the defense and the attackers less. Some more Jap artillery was brought forward as well. Finally, he ordered work to start to widen and clear the track and make it workable for his army.

The Allied forces filled the gap but felt content to consolidate. They'd won a victory for now, and the enemy was in retreat, finally forced on the defensive for a change. Port Moresby was saved.

The whole affair was clamored as a victory in Australia. More than ever, Prime Minister John Curtin was happy that he brought General Douglas MacArthur to command the Southwest theater.

The old and wily General was the man for the situation and had just let the damned Japs know that he wasn't too excited about defense.

EPILOGUE

Imperial General Headquarters (Dai Honei)

<h2 style="text-align:center">Meeting, June 6th, 1942</h2>

Grand Admiral Yamamoto stirred from his bed, still quite tired. He wasn't a youngling anymore, and long trips were not as easy as they used to be. He was in his Tokyo mansion north of the city and had arrived late the evening before. He'd flown directly from Hawaii on a very long voyage, with three stops on the way because of the enormous distances involved.

He flew in on one of Japan's experimental bombers, the Nakajima G5N Shinzan ("Deep Mountain"). It was a four-engine, long-range heavy bomber. In June 1942, only three prototypes were built. Yamamoto had ordered one flown to Hawaii just in case he was recalled to Japan or needed to move around rapidly within the enormous Japanese Empire. The aircraft had an incredible range of 4260 kilometers. While it was beyond the country's capability to build it in great numbers, there wasn't an immediate operational need for it. Still, the plane came in handy for the Grand Admiral when he was recalled to Tokyo for a meeting at the Imperial General Headquarters.

That didn't mean that it was a harrowing flight. Despite the fantastic range, Yamamoto had to stop at Midway (2800 kilometers and 12 hours journey) for refueling, then at Wake Island (another 2500 kilometers further and eleven-hour flight). And then, from Wake, he made the final leg of the voyage to Tokyo directly (3950 kilometers and twenty hours).

Hence the reason he was sore and still tired. He got cleaned, shaved, and had some good food. He then left his mansion for his beautiful garden (the flowers and trees were in full bloom), where a black car awaited him. He got in, and the vehicle sped away to his destination.

The Imperial General Headquarters (Daihon'ei), the Japanese command body responsible for coordinating efforts between the Imperial Japanese Army and Navy during wartime.

The goal of liaison conferences (Dai Honei) was to try and integrate the decisional process for the two branches of the military, the normally bickering Navy and Army. The two halves of the Japanese military did not always work together to attain the state's objective.

But since the start of the war, things had gone surprisingly smoothly. It was not that it had been easy, but both services had followed the plans (more or less) and achieved victory on a scale that was only the stuff of dreams for most Japanese before the conflict.

But lately, things had started to get complicated again, with several minor military setbacks, and the old habits had resurfaced. What had been carefully hidden below a layer of unprecedented successes now came back in full view. The bickering was back.

And so, the Emperor had called the meeting (Yamamoto was sure it was Prime Minister Tojo's initiative), so the Army and Navy could discuss overall strategy.

Isoroku thought about the growing discrepancies in the Imperial force's objectives. He was against an invasion of Australia since it was clear that Japan had already reached the limit of its operational capability. He was already seeing the strain on his naval and air forces. The Army, on the other hand, wanted to attack everywhere. They prepared a campaign in Burma that would ultimately end up attacking India, while they also wanted to land in Australia.

The Grand Admiral had already concluded that the Empire needed time to consolidate the territories and resources it had already absorbed. Also, he firmly believed that the maximum effort should be put toward building up the defenses in Hawaii and the other Pacific islands and continue to push hard in the Coral Sea to prevent the shipping lanes from isolating the Australians.

As he was lost in thoughts, the car stopped by the Imperial Castle. He was directed into the building by a sharp-looking staff officer. He eventually got to the grand and richly decorated meeting room, where Marshal Hajime, the Army commander-in-chief, awaited him. Also, there was Prime Minister Hideki Tojo and Admiral Osami Nagano, one of the top Navy men at HQ. Towering above them all was emperor and living god Hiro-Hito, sitting on his throne, keeping silent as always. He wasn't supposed to intervene in the meeting, just watch and approve the final decisions taken.

The room opened onto a large balcony with a plunging view of Tokyo. The windows were open, a gentle breeze drifted in, and the morning sun ruffled the light silk curtains.

"Ah, Grand Admiral," said Tojo, bowing, sitting up from the central table. The other council members followed him, and Yamamoto did the same. He then specifically bowed low to the Emperor to salute him in his most respectful fashion.

"Have a seat," said Tojo, gesturing to Yamamoto to a chair. "Thank you to all of you for coming to this meeting, especially the Grand Admiral, who had to fly, I am told, over forty hours to get here." Tojo again gave a slight bow of respect to Isoroku. "I have gathered you

here so we can talk about the war's future conduct. There is no question that Japan now reigns supreme in the Pacific and that our enemies are cowering in fear. But Japan's resources are limited, and we must decide what to do." Tojo sat up, gesturing to the junior officer by the door in the back of the room. It opened, and another junior staff officer came in with a large map of the whole Pacific on a wooden stool.

"I don't have to retell you the story of our conquests; you have been the ones directing them, after all. But we need to decide where to strike and how. We have several options on the table." He gestured to Marshal Hajime. "The Army favors a campaign in Burma, an attack in India, and a conquest of Australia." Hajime gave a head nod to signify his approval. Tojo continued. "And continued attacks in China to consolidate our gains and get the Nationalist Chinese to come and sit down to the table for peace."

He then gestured toward Nagano. "The Navy wants to stop attacking, put our forces on a defensive stance, and continue to build up the necessary military forces to repulse the unavoidable American counter-offensive."

"We need to continue attacking. Our forces are victorious, and the enemy is reeling back in disarray. Now is the time to finish him." Marshal Hajime intervened, clearly stating the Army's wish. Nagano calmly looked at him. The two men did not like each other because of an intense rivalry between the Army and the Navy. "Let's have Grand Admiral Yamamoto talk," Tojo answered, looking at the Grand Admiral.

"Gentleman, thank you for having me here and for letting me expose my views on the war's situation and how we should continue prosecuting it," started Isoroku. "While I understand the Army's wish to continue conquering and while I would also like to destroy the Indian and Australians, Japan is not in a position to do so."

Hajime gave him a dark look, and Tojo did as well. Yamamoto understood where the wind was blowing. The Prime Minister seemed to favor the Army's point of view. "We can already see the signs of over-extension of our forces. A defeat near Port Moresby, some naval reverses in the Coral Sea, damaged ships returning to Japan for repairs, ammunition, and supplies issues... The list is long, gentlemen. We have conquered many resources and have significantly expanded our realm. We should concentrate on absorbing those new possessions while building up our Hawaiian and other Pacific Islands' defenses." He paused to look at the Army man. "And anyway, where would we find the troops to invade such large lands?"

Marshall Hajime took a few seconds to answer. "Grand Admiral. Let me assure you that I have the matter of how many divisions I have and where they could be used well in hand. But for the record and for your information, we will be taking the troops from the Kwantung Garrison Army that sits at the Soviet border."

The Kwantung Army was a big army group that maintained a staggering 700,000 men in Manchuria to guard the border with the Soviet Union. Its size was because it needed to be there to deter the USSR from attacking. But the fact remained that the Russians were busy fighting the Nazis in Europe and, as such, had other people to fight against. And besides, the Kwantung Army was the best-equipped and most-trained force in Imperial Japan.

Yamamoto was a little surprised by the marshal's declaration since the Army had always been a proponent of the northern strategy, meaning that it favored an attack and expansion into Russian Siberia and China instead of the attack in the south. He guessed that the recent and incredible success in the Pacific had changed the Army leader's mind. In the end, if the Army liberated the troops for Pacific duty, the Navy could profit from expanding its garrison forces on the newly conquered islands.

"Very well, Marshal," said the Grand Admiral in a neutral tone. "Let me know what you propose. With a large enough body of troops, maybe something can indeed be done about Australia and India...."

Yamamoto played the game, but deep down, he suspected that Japan was stretching it a little too far. The meeting went on for several more hours. In the end, a strategy was agreed upon. An immediate offensive would be launched at Burma to seize its oil and rubber resources (Rangoon), and some probing attacks would be then followed into India. The main Army attack would come from a landing in northwestern Australia and the city of Darwin.

A compromise was also reached to stay on the defensive in New Guinea for the time being and supply the Navy with several dozen battalions to help better garrison and prepare the Pacific Defenses against the incoming American forces.

The day after, Yamamoto flew back immediately toward Hawaii, as he was certain the American forces were approaching an attack date. He also gave the necessary orders to recall the Soryu and Hiryu to Pearl Harbor, anticipating the naval battle he thought would happen soon in or near the Hawaiian Islands. To compensate for the loss of two main fleet carriers to Admiral Inoue's forces, he sent four light carriers to Rabaul, the Shoho, Hiyo, Taiyo, and the newly built Unyo. Altogether they compensated for the same number of embarked planes as the Soryu and Hiryu.

Churchill pays a visit to the troops, mid-May 1942

In Allied-held territory, the beautiful city of Agadir was the epicenter of British and Allied power in the theater. Winston Churchill, the Prime Minister of the United Kingdom and now de facto leader of the British Empire at war, had arrived a couple of days earlier in his dear "courier ship," as he fondly called it, the magnificent battleship Prince of Wales.

Sailing out of Quebec City, Canada, he had embarked on the ship and the great convoy accompanying it to visit Agadir. At this early stage in the war, the Axis did not possess many surface ships or submarines to threaten Allied movements at sea seriously, so the British fleet had not been bothered in the least.

This meant that the war leader had a lot of time to ponder the strategic situation. First, an uninterrupted series of epic disasters had again befallen the Union Jack, this time in Asia. Hong Kong was occupied by the Japs, and the Canadian brigade defending it was destroyed.

The Malay peninsula, Thailand, and ultimately, the great fortress of Singapore had also fallen to the seemingly unstoppable Nipponese forces. Burma would also soon be attacked. To top it all, India would soon be threatened.

However, it was a vast country, and the Indian army was strong, bolstered by British and even some American troops. The Allies maintained a pretty large fleet in the Indian Ocean, blocking the Japanese from getting too bold. No, he had thought soberly, in his cabin in the black of night while the ship slightly rocked over the waves. India would hold. It had to hold.

Then next was Australia. The Japanese forces had landed in New Guinea and Rabaul. They also took the New Hebrides, New Caledonia, and the Fijis. They also finished the conquest of the Dutch East Indies. The country was completely isolated. Things did not look stellar for the Aussies.

He'd discussed the defense of Australia with all of the Empire's constituent countries, and it had been decided that each major army would send some forces whenever the shipping lanes opened up again. The Canadian Army sent one division of French-Canadians, two South African divisions, and one New Zealander. Major fortifications were underway in Darwin, Sydney, Melbourne, and others. All significant roadways would soon be sporting several defensive works if the Japanese ever invaded. The United States was also sending a relief fleet, and Britain would contribute with the Iron Duke battleship, amongst others. The hopes were that the fleet could block the Imperial Navy from doing anything serious. Famous General Macarthur, fresh off the Philippines, had also taken command of the new South Sea Command that was taking place.

What he had been left to think about was the African theater of war since it was the only area in the world where the Allies were able to stand against the Axis for the moment. At that time, it was the only area where the Allies could confidently stand up to the German hordes. Because of the distance involved, the Empire had two cards to play.

First, a limited offensive could be sent against Egypt from Sudan; the Italian army and the small collaborationist Egyptian national army mostly defended that. Four divisions of the Empire, including just one motorized, would probably not accomplish a total conquest of the area, but maybe he would get some victory he could brag about.

Second, and the reason for his voyage to Agadir, was the first serious Allied counter-offensive that would soon be launched on the unsuspecting Axis armies dug in facing the Tiggert-Tikrit defensive line built by the Allies in 1940. The attack would hug the coastline to maximize the impact of the powerful combined fleet sailing on the left flank of the twelve divisions advancing north. It could provide much-needed artillery support with its large guns. The black snake shore-bombardment operation had shown how effective that could be if it had an efficient air cover. The big battlewagons of the fleet could be risked in a sortie against ground troops since they would be protected from air attacks. Indeed, the German Luftwaffe would be there to offer battle, and there would be losses. But it was hoped that the attack would bear some fruits, and the objective was to retake Casablanca and Marrakech.

He'd just landed in the port area after a ten-day trip. British national anthem blazing, honor guard saluting, French Foreign Legion present in their hundreds. He had been welcomed by the theater commander in the area, Bernard Montgomery. A bit too sure of himself for Churchill's tastes, the general nonetheless radiated an air of confidence.

The French leaders, Petain and De Gaulle were also present in Agadir, their temporary capital. The French hadn't been so lucky to have strong colonies to rebase and rebuild their armies. So, they were stuck with what was left of their African empire and American help. They had welcomed the leader of the British Empire with great fanfare and pomp.

After the parties and welcome came the unavoidable meetings. Discussions in which he had had to strong-arm the two French leaders into accepting the principle of Anglo-Saxons commanding the offensive in their own empire.

After all, he had concluded with his last convincing argument the French only brought one division to the offensive, sporting American equipment. In the end, the proud French relented. Montgomery would drive the show.

And today, he was currently busy reviewing troops in one of the main assembly areas of the town. He was shaking hands, tapping shoulders, having quick talks of encouragement, and having solemn eye contact with the soldiers. All the while, he listened to the pompous general describe which unit it was, what they had done, and so on.

He was going through the motions, doing what a politician does best. But at the same time, he was also lost in thought, still pondering the problems of the empire. He needed a victory. Hell, the Allies needed a win. Would he get one in the offensive scheduled for the end of May?

Washington D.C., May 30th, 1942

What was evident from a cursory look at the map was that the Axis powers held the best hand. From the Pacific islands to North Africa and now into Russia, the Fascists' armies were reigning supreme.

But appearances could be deceiving, President Roosevelt thought. The Japanese Empire had no way of knowing what giant they had awakened. Whatever little resistance there still was about his sole decision to take the country to war against the Germans was now gone. There were no restraints. No more isolationist factions in the USA. American vengeance would rain down on its enemies wherever they chose to stand.

The meeting had just concluded with General Marshall, the commander-in-chief of the Armed forces, and Admiral King, the head of the U.S. Navy. A course for the strategy in the Pacific had been set. They first found a fleet to sail to Australia to help hold against the Japanese tide. Then, Two carriers, the Wasp and Yorktown, were cruising at top speed toward the Panama Canal to join up with the two battleship divisions that had missed Pearl Harbor because they had been sent to the Atlantic in 1940. The carrier Hornet was already in the Pacific, in San Diego. A French contingent also arrived with two battleships, five cruisers, and twenty support ships. They would join up with the 2nd fleet, comprised of the new vessels of the Navy that had been built since 1941, amongst others, a brand-new battleship, several cruisers, and destroyers.

A total of seven battleships, five aircraft carriers, twenty heavy cruisers and light cruisers, and forty destroyers would form the nucleus of Task Force 1 and 2. The naval groupings would be the fleets for the first American counterstroke in the Pacific theater. The obvious target was the Hawaiian Islands, held by the Japanese Empire since March 1942. It was reported that the enemy had substantially fortified and reinforced the island chain. According to the OSS (the U.S. Intelligence Service), eight Imperial Army divisions were now in the islands. One on Kauai, one on Maui, two on the Big Island, and four on Oahu, where Honolulu and Pearl Harbor were located. Numerous smaller units were also occupying the smaller islands in the chain.

Unknown to Tokyo and the rest of the world, the Americans had broken Japanese naval codes, so they could pretty much read the Imperial Navy's secret communication when they could intercept them, which was quite often. The reports were that a substantial naval force was based in the area. If these reports could be believed, Yamato itself was moored in Pearl, with six other battleships: Hiei, Kongo, Nagato, Kirishima, and Mutsu. Almost all of the Kiddo Butai, the Japanese aircraft carrier force, was also based there, representing four top-of-the-line ships (Kaga, Akagi, Shokaku, and Zuikaku) with tons of ace pilots. Dozens of air squadrons were also strewn about in all of Hawaii's airfields. It was a powerful Japanese presence.

The island chain was the key to any American offensive in the Pacific. Without it, there was nothing to be done; the distances involved were too great. So, any U.S. attacks would first need to be directed there. And Japs knew it as well, Roosevelt thought.

Well, there was no helping it; it had to be a predictable attack, which is why Admiral King had proposed sending the most powerful fleet the USA could field in 1942. The goal was not yet to land and retake the islands but more or less to find and engage the Imperial Navy. Perhaps they could destroy or severely deplete it, forcing the enemy to rebase some of its fleets to Japan or elsewhere in the Pacific.

Speaking of the Japanese strategic mastermind, the presence of the Yamato super-battleship meant that the admiral in charge of the Imperial Navy was also there since it was his reported headquarters and the fleet's flagship. It made sense to Roosevelt, as this was the critical decision point in the Pacific War. The Japanese leader needed to be close to the action. He resolved to talk some more about this later.

"General Marshall, what are the dispositions for the Agadir offensive in Africa?" He said. "Mr. President, this should be a Franco-British show, apart from the few naval units we committed to the operation," the general said, pausing to take a sip of the coffee that a good-looking orderly had placed in front of him a minute earlier. "We have not added any troops to the area. As you know, Mr. President, we are still rebuilding after the severe defeats in the Middle East last year," he finished, looking at King for more details.

"I concur with General Marshall, Mr. President," said King, in his stern tone that was characteristic of his personality. "The French and British have enough big guns to support the attack sufficiently. The British also have three excellent carriers with which to cover the fleet, while land-based planes should do the rest," finished the admiral in a confident tone. "Thank you for these details, gentlemen," he added, tapping nonchalantly with his fingers on the desk. "And what of Churchill?" "The Prime minister arrived in Agadir two days ago and is currently reviewing the troops," said Marshall, reading thru a report saying as much. "Yes, old Winston would love a victory," said Roosevelt with a thin smile. He liked the old warhorse.

The leader of the British Empire was the type of man anyone wanted in a scrap. And he was happy to have him on his side. Marshall then described what the coming offensive would face in the area. "The Axis has about five divisions facing Franco-brits and several more in the rear. But the high component of Italo-Spanish troops can give us some prospects for victory. However, The two German divisions in the area are solid veterans of the French and North African campaign, and the enemy has a lot of air strength, not counting a ton of artillery dug in in pretty good defensive positions," finished Marshall, again shuffling thru the papers, reading the figures as he was speaking. "Well, let's hope for the best, gentlemen," rapidly said Roosevelt in a tone that meant the subject was closed.

"Now, general, let's talk about those production figures and the new ships about to be launched...." The meeting continued for several more hours. They talked about the allocation of resources, the naval pilot training program (they would need a lot of them to man the 200 planned aircraft carriers of all sizes that would be built in the next four to five years), and the organizing of several armored divisions for an eventual offensive into Europe itself.

They eventually talked about an exciting subject to the President since he was a fan of the Big naval guns, even if they were juggernauts from a bygone age. From his point of view, if the Japs had them, then America needed to build bigger, better, and in larger numbers.

"What of the planned Montana-Class battleships program," asked the president in an interested tone. The new breed of U.S. battlewagons, approved to be built by Congress in 1938, was the American response to the Yamato-Class, already in construction at the time. Five ships were approved for construction. The vessels would sport 76,000 tons at full load and 407mm (16.5 in) guns. Admiral King joined in, having a lot more details for the President:

"There are serious talks of canceling the program, Mr. President," he said with a severe face. "How come?" the genuine surprise could be read on Roosevelt's face. "We believe that carriers are the way to go in the future, so it might be better to use the allocated resources to build ships that will be more useful." Roosevelt cut him off by talking right away to prevent the admiral from talking more. "Is that so?" he said hesitantly. "Build me at least one of them," he said in a commanding voice.

Both Marshall and King knew better than to argue with the President when he had this tone. They would build at least one of them. King thought for a moment that while they were at it, he should also hope for Montana to face up with a Yamato-Class in this war. Why not, since they would have one anyway?

The rest of the meeting was filled with talks about the future planned operation to retake the British Islands. Being more a project than an operation, they discussed it in general terms and the needed resources to make it happen.

THE PACIFIC ALTERNATE SERIE WILL CONTINUE IN THE SECOND BOOK :
BATTLE PACIFIC

*** Please visit my new website

*** Please review my book(s) on Amazon and Goodreads.com.

*** It really helps me out and motivates me to write more books. Many thanks for considering my request.

*** Send me an email at souvorov@hotmail.com if you feel like chatting about the books of the story.

Thank you very much for reading my work.

I HAVE A NEW FACEBOOK PAGE! PLEASE GO AND VISIT:

https://www.facebook.com/profile.php?id=61558770082344

*** Please review my book(s) on Amazon and Goodreads.com and try not to be a troll.

.

*** Send me an email at **souvorov@hotmail.com** if you feel like chatting with me. **I respond to every email.**

Some of the books that I have unpublished are for sale on:

www.maxlamirande.com

THE BLITZKRIEG ALTERNATE SERIES

BY MAX LAMIRANDE

Book 1: Blitzkrieg Europa – 2nd Edition – fall 2024

Book 2: Battle Europa 2nd Edition – fall 2024

Book 3: Struggle Europa 2nd Edition – winter 2024

Book 4: Fortress Europa 2nd Edition – winter 2024

Book 5: Stalemate Europa 2nd Edition – winter 2024

Book 6: Staggering Europa 2nd Edition – spring 2024

Book 7: Faltering Europa 2nd Edition – spring 2024

Book 8: Crumbling Europa 2nd Edition – spring 2024

Book 9: Falling Europa 2nd Edition – TBD

Book 10: Soviet Europa 2nd Edition – TBD

Book 11: Red Europa 2nd Edition – TBD

Book 12: Climax Europa 2nd Edition – TBD

Book 13: The Walder Chronicles Part 1

Book 14: The Walder Chronicles Part 2

Book 15: The Walder Chronicles Part 3

THE PACIFIC ALTERNATE SERIES

BY MAX LAMIRANDE

THE NAPOLEONIC ALTERNATE SERIES

BY MAX LAMIRANDE

Book 1: *Austerlitz Alternate*

Book 2: *Friedland Alternate*

Book 3: 1809 Alternate – Winter 2025

THE AXIS ALTERNATE SERIES

BY MAX LAMIRANDE

THE GREAT WAR ALTERNATE SERIES

BY MAX LAMIRANDE

Book 1: *Schlieffen Alternate*

Book 2: *Great War Alternate (Summer-Fall 2024)*

Book 3: *1915 Alternate*

Book 4:

Book 5:

Book 6:

Also, from the same author:

AUSTERLITZ ALTERNATE

DECEMBER 2ND, 1805

The War of the Third Coalition rages in Europe. Battles have been fought, and Napoleon Bonaparte's Grande Armée sweeps everything before it. After a big victory over an Austrian Army in Ulm, the French occupied Vienna, the capital of the Austrian Empire.

The Russians entered Austria to come to the help of their Allies and under pressure from the British. The Austro-Russians and the French are about to clash in a small, unknown town called Austerlitz.

And then everything changes. The French stop trying to retake the Pratzen Heights, and the day's battle ends in a stalemate for both armies. Kutusov, the allied army's leader in the absence of young Tsar Alexander (who fell ill and is still somewhere in Galicia), decides to retire the army northward with the Austrian Emperor's approval.

The news galvanizes the Revolution's enemies and of the Empire, jealous of Napoleon's success and wanting him gone. The Prussians decide to join the war and move their troops into Austria to link their forces with the two other powers. The German states and other countries like Naples rethink their stances in the conflict. And the French Emperor's internal enemies, ever-wishing the old regime's return, start plotting to overthrow the government in Paris.

All the while, the Ottoman Empire, convinced by the French several months earlier to enter the war, has decided to intervene in favor of Bonaparte and invade southern Hungary with an Army. Austria is on the brink of annihilation, but Napoleon's Grande Armée also has a big challenge ahead since it now needs to defeat three major powers simultaneously.

Everything will come down to either Napoleon's genius to overcome the odds and win regardless of the troops arrayed against him or his defeat and the end of the French Empire.

This is the story of the Napoleonic Wars.

Also, from the same author:

SCHLIEFFEN ALTERNATE

Europe, August 1914.

The World explode into war as Austro-Hungary declares war on Serbia following the assassination of the heir to the throne, Archduke Franz Ferdinand. Russia follows suit and mobilizes, while Germany supports its ally and declares war on Russia. France then joins the conflict as it is Russia's ally.

The British intervene when the Germans execute their Schlieffen Plan and attack through Belgium to outflank the French defenses. And then pandemonium explodes everywhere. The Austro-Hungarian attack in Serbia and Galicia, the Russians invade Prussia, and the Germans smash into France. In the Middle East, the Ottoman Empire declares for the Central Power, while Italy stays neutral.

The German Army is unstoppable and closes in on Paris as the Allies retreat in disarray all along the front. The fate of the World hangs in the balance as a big battle looms for Paris. However, no gains come without giving something away. While the German Army is busy conquering the French and beating the British Expeditionary Force around, the Russians storm Prussia and roll over the German 8th Army. The Reich has all of its remaining troops fighting in the West and nothing fresh to put in front of the Russian steamroller. Koenigsberg fall and the Austro-Hungarians fail before Belgrade and in Galicia. Something will have to be done, or else Berlin will fall to the Russian Imperial forces.

This is the story of a war that might have been.

Also, from the same author:

THE BEAR AND THE SWASTIKA

The year is 1939.

The World rocks with the news of the signing of the Germano-Soviet pact. A dark veil soon falls on Europe as Poland is invaded and destroyed by the overwhelming forces of the Wehrmacht and the Red Army.

France and the United Kingdom can only sit by and watch the two military juggernauts obliterate the Polish state. No one believes the two totalitarian regimes can agree in the long term as their ideologies completely contradict each other.

Russia wants influence in the Balkans, has eyes on Finland, and wants an opening to the Mediterranean. Germany needs Romanian oil to keep its war machine operational, and Hitler is adamant about not letting the Bolsheviks gain another inch of ground in Europe. At least not more than he has already given out in the treaty of non-aggression signed before the Polish campaign.

The year is 1940.

The French campaign then unfolds with a disaster for the Allies, and the Germans win an incredible victory over the combined forces of the United Kingdom and France. British forces narrowly escape to their island with the remnants of their armies, and France surrenders. Half of the country is occupied by the Germans. It seems that the swastika will conquer the world, especially with the Russian bear watching its back.

Germano-Soviet Axis talks were organized in October 1940 concerning the Soviet Union's potential entry as a fourth Axis Power during World War II. The negotiations include a two-day conference in Berlin between

Soviet Foreign Minister Vyacheslav Molotov, Adolf Hitler, and German Foreign Minister Joachim von Ribbentrop. The two powers will try to agree on a formal alliance to divide the world.

The fate of liberty hangs in the balance.

Also from the same Author:

BLITZKRIEG EUROPA – 2ND EDITION

September 1st, 1939.

Germany invades Poland, igniting a major European war. A few months later, the French are also invaded, and the allied armies are utterly defeated. Then the Dunkirk disaster happens, and the United Kingdom loses most of its land army. Soon, the British Isles are also attacked, and the British are hard-pressed with a serious German invasion. The French struggle to resist the Axis forces bent on conquering all of their mainland home country and West African colonies. Watching from its safe shores, America cannot stay still while Western Europe and all of the Mediterranean fall to the forces of the Axis. And when the Afrika Corps plunges over the Suez and invades the Middle East, the Soviet Union finally decides to join.

And through it all, a hero emerges. Erich Walder, tank commander, will have to fight on all fronts and attempt to survive what the enemy will throw at him.

This is the story of the Second World War.

Also, from the same author:

SPACE WAR, An Empire Divided

The Empire built by Haakon the Great is no more. It's 4124, and the Human race has spread to the stars in four different star clusters by discovering light speed and wormholes. A civil war has broken out between the different human enclaves to see who will be the next emperor of humanity.

The Ptolemy and Hadesian Star Nations are invading Elysium, allied with New America from the Alpha Perseis Cluster. Large battles are being fought in star systems between former comrades of the Imperial Fleet. In space, battleships unload their powerful weapons at each other while giant battle mechas fight for control of the ground.

The opportunity is too great for the evil Cybernetic forces in the Caldwell 14 Star Cluster. Having fought – and lost – a terrible war against the Empire two hundred years ago, they are gathering for a return engagement against humanity.

A thousand years before, Haakon has dreamed and foreseen a terrible time for humanity. The Black Death is coming to consume all, and his Empire will not be there to fight it.

www.ingramcontent.com/pod-product-compliance
Lightning Source LLC
Chambersburg PA
CBHW071559030726
47593CB00001BA/232